Theory & Harmony
for the Contemporary Musician

by Arnie Berle

A practical guide to essential knowledge for today's musician. A full course covering everything from the fundamentals of sound and music notation to popular song forms and chord scales for improvisation.

Amsco Publications
New York/London/Sydney

Cover photography by Randall Wallace
Interior design and layout by Len Vogler

This book Copyright © 1996 by Amsco Publications,
A Division of Music Sales Corporation, New York

Order No. AM 931360
US International Standard Book Number: 0.8256.1499.6
UK International Standard Book Number: 0.7119.5137.3

Exclusive Distributors:
Music Sales Corporation
257 Park Avenue South, New York, NY 10010 USA
Music Sales Limited
8/9 Frith Street, London W1V 5TZ England
Music Sales Pty. Limited
120 Rothschild Street, Rosebery, Sydney, NSW 2018, Australia

Printed in the United States of America by
Vicks Lithograph and Printing Corporation

Contents

PREFACE

Music theory is that branch of music that deals with the principles and methods of making music. *Harmony* is that branch of music that deals with the simultaneous sounding of three or more notes called *chords* which are used to accompany a melody in a pleasing and satisfying way. Of course it is possible to play an instrument very well without any knowledge of theory or harmony. There are many people who have great ears, a good sense of rhythm, and very highly developed physical skills all of which are required to play an instrument well. So why study theory or harmony? Music has been called a language. When we study a language we can just learn the vocabulary by rote and manage to speak conversationally quite well. But to really know a language, to be able to read and write in that language, you must study the grammar of that language. That is why we study theory and harmony. It helps us to write music better, to explain our music better to other musicians, to see and hear relationships between notes and chords better, to have a better understanding of all kinds of music. In other words, we study theory and harmony because it makes us better musicians than just instrumentalists.

TO THE STUDENT

This book starts at the very elementary level and proceeds very gradually to the most advanced level of theory. You should start anyplace in the book where you feel your knowledge is lacking or needs some strengthening. Be sure to use the worksheets that are provided throughout the book. They will help you to measure your progress. Some instrumental exercises are also provided to be practiced on your instrument. These exercises will provide some practical application of the theory that you are learning. So go slow, have fun, and remember: "straight ahead."

FUNDAMENTALS OF SOUND · MUSICAL NOTATION

Before we begin our study of music theory and harmony, it is important that we have an understanding of a basic ingredient of music; that is, *sound*. All musical compositions are simply the organization of the properties that make up sound, namely, *pitch, dynamics, timbre,* and *duration*.

SOUND

Sound is the sensation of vibrating air stimulating the auditory nerves. These vibrations may be caused by the motion of air produced by the plucking of a string (piano, guitar, violin), or the beating of a drumhead.

PITCH

Pitch is the highness or lowness of sound. The pitch is determined by the number of sound waves produced per second. The greater the number, the higher the pitch or sound. The lower the number, the lower the sound.

Pitch is indicated by a system of notation in which certain kinds of symbols called *notes* are placed on a series of five lines called a *staff*. Below is a staff with notes placed on the lines or in the spaces between the lines. The lower the note is on the staff, the lower the pitch of the note. The higher the note is on the staff, the higher the pitch.

DYNAMICS

Dynamics refers to the loudness or softness of the sound. Composers use certain words derived from the Italian language to indicate the gradations of loudness or softness at various points in a composition.

Symbol	In Italian	Indicates
pp	pianissimo	very soft
mp	mezzo piano	moderately soft
mf	mezzo forte	moderately loud
f	forte	loud
ff	fortissimo	very loud

TIMBRE

Timbre is that characteristic quality of a sound that distinguishes one instrument from another. The timbre of the clarinet, for example, is that quality of the clarinet sound that enables us to distinguish it from the oboe or any other instrument.

DURATION

Duration refers to the length of time a pitch or a note is sounded. Below is a table listing the duration of different kinds of notes. Notice that each note has a corresponding symbol for a rest that indicates a period of silence: you do not play through the rest.

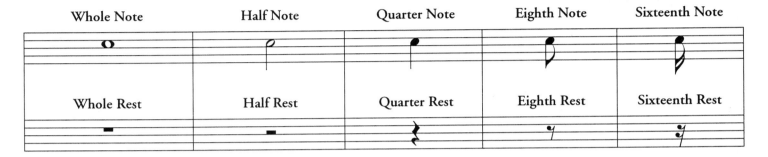

Whole Note	Half Note	Quarter Note	Eighth Note	Sixteenth Note
Whole Rest	Half Rest	Quarter Rest	Eighth Rest	Sixteenth Rest

TIME SIGNATURE

The *time signature* is a set of two numbers placed at the beginning of a staff that divides a piece of music into groupings of counts. Each grouping of counts is called a measure. Below is an example of a time signature.

4 The top number indicates the number of counts or beats in each measure.

4 The bottom number indicates which note duration receives one count. For example, if the number 4 is on the bottom, it means that the quarter note receives one count. If the number eight is the bottom number, then the eighth note receives one count.

The following table lists the count value of the different kinds of note durations when the bottom number of the time signature is 4.

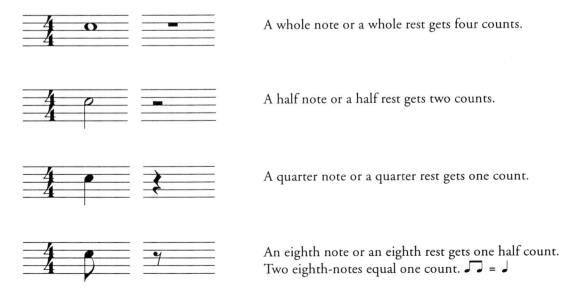

A whole note or a whole rest gets four counts.

A half note or a half rest gets two counts.

A quarter note or a quarter rest gets one count.

An eighth note or an eighth rest gets one half count.
Two eighth-notes equal one count. ♫ = ♩

A sixteenth note or a sixteenth rest gets one quarter count. Four sixteenth-notes equal one count.

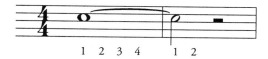

THE TIE

The *tie* is a curved line connecting two notes of the same pitch. The time value of the second note is added on to the value of the first note.

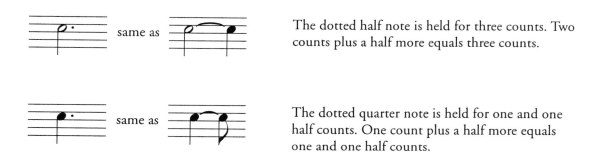

The first note is held for a total of six counts by adding on the value of the second note. Or, four counts plus two more counts.

THE DOT

The *dot* placed next to a note increases the value of that note by one half.

The dotted half note is held for three counts. Two counts plus a half more equals three counts.

The dotted quarter note is held for one and one half counts. One count plus a half more equals one and one half counts.

THE CLEF

The *clef* is a symbol placed at the beginning of a staff that establishes the letter names of the lines and spaces of the staff.

Treble Clef (G Clef)

The *treble* or *G clef* is placed at the beginning of a staff and indicates that a note placed on the second line of that staff would have the letter name of G. All the other notes would then be named relative to that G.

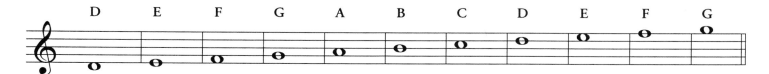

Bass Clef (F Clef)

The *bass* or *F clef* is placed at the beginning of a staff and indicates that a note placed on the fourth line of that staff would have the letter name of F. All the other notes would then be named relative to that F.

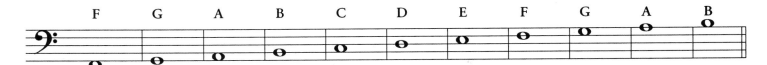

LEGER LINES

For pitches that go beyond the limits of the staff, little *leger lines* are added above or below the staff lines. These added lines can then accommodate the new note.

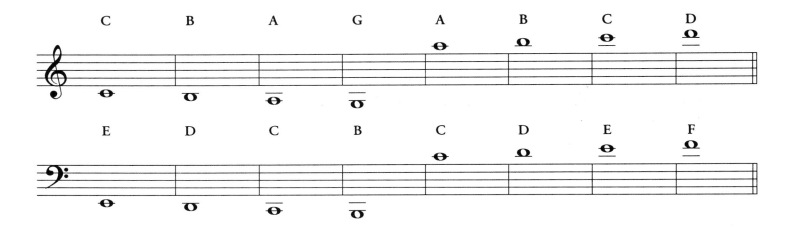

WORKSHEET

1. Write in the letter name of each note on the following staff.

2. Write in the letter name of each note on the following staff.

3. Write in the time signature for each of the following melodies.

CONCLUSION

Now that we have reviewed these fundamentals, we will move ahead to our study of pop and jazz theory. Be sure to complete all worksheets before going on to the next area of study. To gain the most from this text, it would be wise also to play through all the suggested instrumental studies.

HALF STEPS • WHOLE STEPS • MAJOR KEYS

STEPS

A half step is the distance from one note to the very next note, either up or down. This is best understood by looking at a piano keyboard. We can see that a half step occurs between a white note and the next nearest black note, or between a black note and the next nearest white note. The only exceptions are the white note E to the white note F and, the white note B to the white note C.

A whole step is two consecutive half steps. On the keyboard we see that a whole step is the distance from one note to another, skipping a note (black or white) in between.

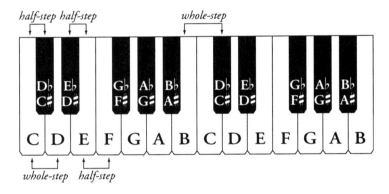

Sharps—Flats—Naturals
1. A sharp (♯) raises a note a half step.
2. A flat (♭) lowers a note a half step.
3. A double sharp (𝄪) raises a note a whole step.
4. A double flat (♭♭) lowers a note a whole step.
5. A natural (♮) cancels out a previous sharp or flat.

Double sharps and double flats are generally avoided in pop and jazz writings. The *enharmonic note*, which is just another way of spelling a note, is used in place of the double sharp or double flat.

KEYS

A key is a group of notes or tones all related to one common note called the *keynote* or the *tonic*. The keynote names the key.

Key of C   **Key of G**

keynote   keynote

Notice how the notes that make up the little melody in each of the above keys all relate to and gravitate to their keynote.

MAJOR SCALES

A *scale* is a succession of notes in a particular key arranged in a definite pattern of whole steps and half steps.

A major scale always follows the pattern of whole steps and half steps shown below.

C major scale

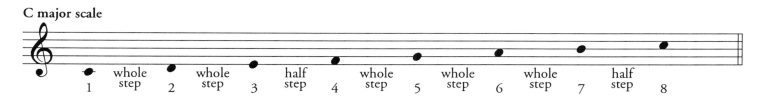

It is very important to remember that in *all* major scales the half steps occur between the third and fourth scale tones and the seventh and eighth scale tones. All other notes are a whole step apart.

A major scale may begin on any note as long as you maintain the pattern shown above. In order to do this, it is necessary to use sharps or flats. Whether you use a sharp or a flat depends on the fact that you must use consecutive letters of the alphabet in creating the scale. For example, when creating a major scale on the note F, the note on the third step of the scale is A; therefore, the next note in the scale is called B♭, not A♯. Calling the note B♭ and not A♯ preserves the consecutive order of the notes in the scale. Notice that the last note of the scale is the same letter as the first note.

F major scale

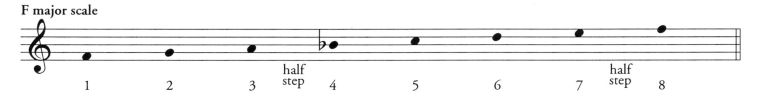

The B♭ is used to maintain the half-step distance between the third and fourth scale tones and also to continue the consecutive sequence of the letter names of the notes.

Below is the G major scale. Notice that an F♯ is used for the seventh scale tone instead of a G♭ in order to keep the consecutive order of the letter names of the notes. The F♯ is also used to create a whole step up from the sixth scale tone and in turn establish the half step up to the eighth scale tone.

G major scale

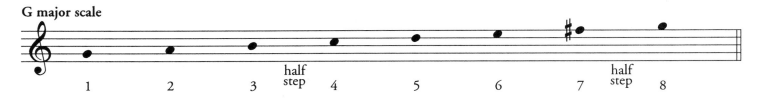

TETRACHORDS

Another method of constructing major scales is to think of the scale as being divided into two equal halves; the first half (lower half) being the scale tones one to four and the second half (the upper half), scale tones five to eight. Each half of the scale is called a *tetrachord*. Each tetrachord is constructed in the following pattern: whole step–whole step–half step. The two tetrachords are separated by a whole step.

C major scale

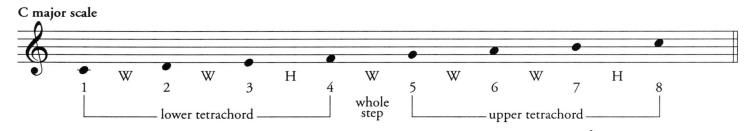

Notice that the two tetrachords have exactly the same construction and are separated by a whole step.

KEYS WITH SHARPS

The C major scale is the only major scale that does not require any sharps or flats to maintain its pattern of whole steps and half steps.

By following the concept of the tetrachord method we can see how sharps and flats are added to form all of the other major scales. For example, the upper tetrachord of the C major scale becomes the lower tetrachord of the next major scale. By adding an upper tetrachord we have the first major scale which requires a sharp. The new scale is the G major scale.

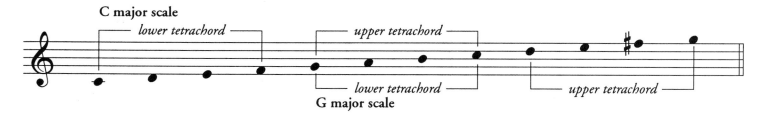

Note that the upper tetrachord of the G scale requires a sharp in order to maintain the whole step–whole step–half step rule for the tetrachord.

To see how the next scale is formed we use the upper tetrachord of the G major scale to become the lower tetrachord of the next scale. By attaching an upper tetrachord we now have the D major scale with two sharps.

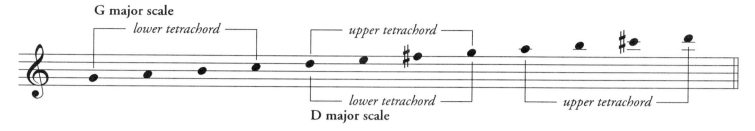

The above principle may be used to construct all the rest of the major scales requiring sharps.

KEYS WITH FLATS

You may have noticed that all major keys requiring sharps follow a certain order: one sharp, the key of G; two sharps, key of D; three sharps, key of A; *etc.* Each new scale begins on the *fifth* note of the previous scale. However, a whole new order of keys may be formed starting on the *fourth* note of a previous scale; for example, starting on the fourth note, F, of the C major scale. By starting on the F and building our tetrachords we form the F major scale.

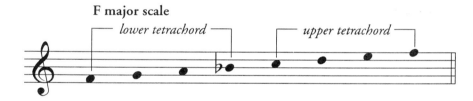

The key of F major has one flat, B♭. The next key in the order of flats begins on the fourth note of the F scale, which is B♭. The new scale is the B♭ major scale, which contains B♭ and E♭.

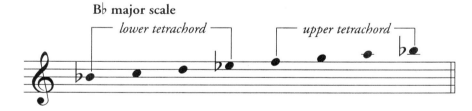

Beginning on the fourth note of the B♭ scale we have the next scale in the order of flats, the E♭ scale, which contains B♭, E♭, and A♭.

By continually starting on the fourth note of the previous scale we can form all of the major keys with flats.

Key Signatures

The sharps and flats that are used in the construction of a particular scale or key are called the *key signature*. The key signature is placed at the beginning of a composition (at the left of the staff next to the clef) and eliminates the need to place the sharp or flat next to those notes in the composition.

The key signature of the F major scale or any composition written in the key of F is one flat, B♭. It indicates that any B in the piece is played as a B♭. (Note the flat signs in brackets.) It is not necessary to place the flat sign next to every B.

The key signature of the G major scale or any composition written in the key of G is one sharp, F♯. It indicates that any F in the piece is played as a F♯.

Order of Keys

Below is the order in which the keys increase in the number of sharps or flats.

Sharp Keys

Flat Keys

ENHARMONIC KEYS

Notes that sound the same but are spelled differently are called *enharmonic notes*. Below are several examples.

Scales or keys may also be enharmonic to each other; for example, the F♯ major scale sounds the same as the G♭ major scale, although each scale is spelled differently.

Other enharmonic scales or keys are the C♯ major scale and the D♭ major scale, and the B major scale and the C♭ major scale.

KEY SIGNATURES AND NATURALS

A *natural sign* cancels out any sharp or flat shown in the key signature. The natural applies only to those notes on the same line or space and only within that measure.

Note: The natural next to the C in the first measure does not apply to the C in the second measure. The natural next to the F in the second measure does not apply to the F in the third measure. The sharp placed next to the C in the third measure must be used, otherwise, the preceding natural would also apply to this C note.

KEY SIGNATURES WITH ACCIDENTALS

A sharp, flat, or natural not shown in the key signature is called an *accidental* or a *chromatic tone*. The accidental affects only the note or notes on the same line or space and is canceled out by the barline.

CHROMATIC SCALES

A *chromatic scale* is a scale that is constructed of all half steps. It may ascend using sharps and descend using flats. The scale takes its name from whatever note it starts on.

C Chromatic Scale

G Chromatic Scale

WORKSHEET

1. Write the enharmonic equivalent of the following notes.

2. Draw in a note a half step higher than the given note.

3. Draw in a note a whole step higher than the given note.

4. Construct the following major scales. Place the sharps or flats next to each note rather than using key signatures.

Minor Scales

All major scales have a relative minor scale. The sixth tone of the major scale becomes the first tone (*tonic* or *keynote*) of the relative minor scale. The new scale is called the *natural* or *pure minor scale*.

Notice that the half steps now occur between the second and third tones and the fifth and sixth tones. The key signature of the minor scale is the same as the key signature of the relative major scale. The key signature of the key of C major is no sharps or flats; therefore, the key signature of A minor is also no sharps or flats.

The Harmonic Minor Scale

Another form of the minor scale is called the *harmonic minor scale*. This scale is formed by raising by a half step the seventh tone of the natural minor scale. Notice where the half steps occur in this new scale.

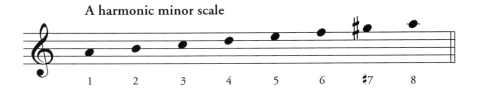

The Melodic Minor Scale

Still another form of the minor scale is the melodic minor scale. This scale is formed by raising by a half step the sixth and seventh tones of the natural minor scale as it ascends. The natural minor scale is used for descending.

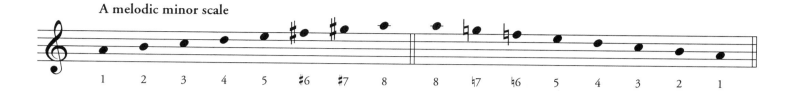

A melodic minor scale

THE PARALLEL MINOR SCALE

The *parallel minor scale* is a minor scale constructed from the same keynote as a major scale. For example, C minor is the parallel minor of the C major scale since both scales are built from the same keynote, C.

Note: The C minor scale shown above is the natural minor scale; however, the C harmonic minor scale and the C melodic minor scale are also parallel minor scales of C major.

THE JAZZ MINOR SCALE (MINOR-MAJOR SCALE)

The *jazz minor scale,* also called the *minor-major scale,* is used by many jazz musicians for reasons that we will learn later in the book. The scale is actually the ascending part of the melodic minor scale (see above). The scale descends in the same manner as it ascends.

An easy and practical way of thinking of the jazz minor scale is to think of the parallel major scale and just lower the third. For example, the A jazz minor scale is the A major scale with the third lowered a half step.

Another example showing the C jazz minor formed from the C major scale.

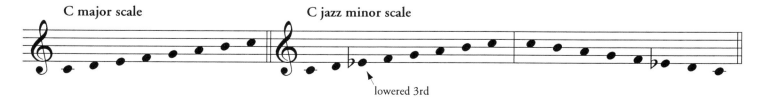

WORKSHEET

Write out the following assorted minor scales.

E harmonic minor scale

E♭ melodic minor scale

B melodic minor scale

A♭ jazz minor scale

A jazz minor scale

D♭ natural minor scale

D natural minor scale

F♯ harmonic minor scale

G harmonic minor scale

B jazz minor scale

C melodic minor scale

C harmonic minor scale

F jazz minor scale

E♭ jazz minor scale

B♭ harmonic minor scale

A natural minor scale

SUGGESTED INSTRUMENTAL EXERCISES

1. Practice and memorize all harmonic minor and jazz minor scales.
2. Make up little melodies based on each of the harmonic minor and jazz minor scales.
   Each melody should occupy two or four measures.

INTERVALS

An *interval* is the distance from one note to another note. Count the lower note as one and count up to the higher note. For example, C to A is a sixth.

C	D	E	F	G	A
1	2	3	4	5	6

Another example, G to C is a fourth.

G	A	B	C
1	2	3	4

There are two kinds of intervals, *harmonic* and *melodic*. Harmonic intervals are two notes played simultaneously; melodic intervals are two notes played consecutively.

Below are more examples of harmonic intervals.

Below are the intervals contained in the major scale.

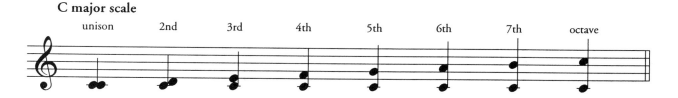

Note that the word *octave* is used in place of eighth.

Major Intervals

The intervals we've seen so far have been determined numerically (second, third, fourth, *etc.*), but intervals may also be described by their quality, such as major, minor, or perfect. Below we see all the major intervals in the C major scale.

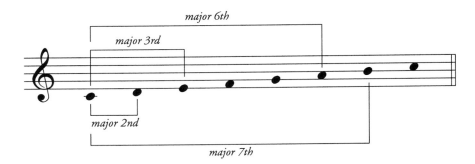

The major intervals are shown here as melodic intervals. Below are the same major intervals shown harmonically. Each upper note of the interval is shown in relation to the keynote.

To determine whether an interval is major, think of the lower note as the temporary keynote of a major scale. If the upper note is in the same scale and forms either a second, third, sixth or seventh, the interval is major. Here are several examples.

Perfect Intervals

Below we see the *perfect* intervals (melodic) derived from the C major scale.

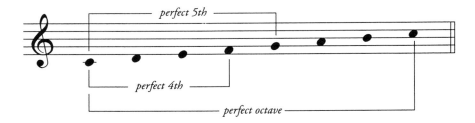

The same perfect intervals are shown harmonically. Notice that the unison is also perfect.

To determine whether an interval is perfect, think of the lower note as the temporary keynote of a major scale. If the upper note is in the same scale and forms either a fourth or fifth or an octave, the interval is perfect. Notice that when two notes sound the same pitch they are said to be in unison.

Below are examples of determining perfect intervals.

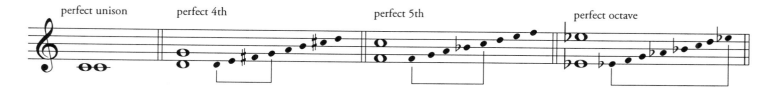

INTERVALS LARGER THAN AN OCTAVE

Intervals may be larger than an octave. Below is an extended C major scale showing the larger intervals related melodically to the keynote C.

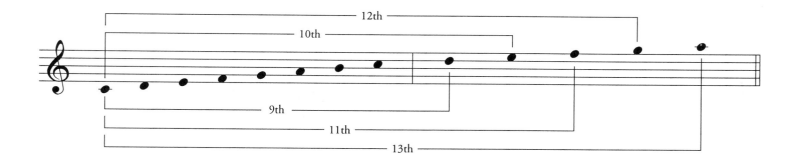

Here are the same intervals shown harmonically in relation to the keynote C.

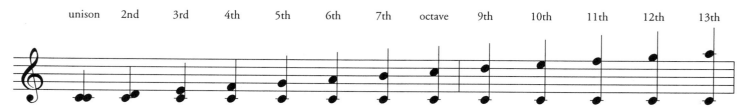

Notice that the intervals that are larger than an octave are of the same quality as the intervals formed when the upper note is an octave lower. For example, C to D is a major second; therefore, C to the D a ninth higher is a major ninth. C to E is a major third; therefore, C to E a tenth higher is a major tenth.

ALTERED INTERVALS

The quality of all intervals may be altered according to the following rules:

To change a major interval to a *minor* interval:
  Lower the upper note a half step.

Raise the lower note a half step.

To change a minor interval to a *major* interval:
  Raise the upper note a half step.

Lower the lower note a half step.

To change a minor or perfect interval to a *diminished* interval:
  Lower the upper note a half step.

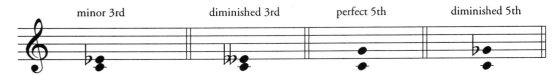

Raise the lower note a half step.

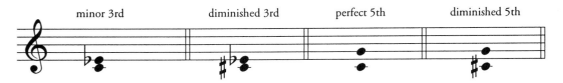

To change a major or perfect interval to an augmented interval:
Raise the upper note a half step.

Lower the lower note a half step.

The numerical name of an interval does not change when the quality of the interval changes. For example, the interval C to E is a major third, C to E♯ is also a third, an augmented third. Do not be confused by the fact that E♯ sounds like an F. The number of the interval is determined by counting the actual letters of the interval and not the enharmonic equivalent. In other words, count from C to E and not C to F, F being the enharmonic equivalent of E♯.

Naming intervals that are heard can be confusing since certain pairs of intervals that are named differently sound the same. For example, C to F♯ (an augmented fourth) sounds the same as C to G♭ (a diminished fifth). Similarly, C to A is a major sixth and sounds the same as C to B♭♭, which is a diminished seventh. However, it is true that using enharmonic equivalents does make things easier. For example, a chord called a diminished seventh (°7) contains a diminished seventh from the root to the highest note, as in a C°7 (C E♭ G♭ B♭♭). But in many cases you will see the notes of the C°7 written as C E♭ G♭ A. If you know that the A is a enharmonic equivalent of B♭♭, you can understand why the chord is named C diminished seventh.

INVERTED INTERVALS

Turning an interval upside down is called *inverting* the interval.

When inverted, major intervals become minor, minor intervals become major, perfect intervals remain perfect, diminished intervals become augmented, and augmented intervals become diminished.

Note that when an interval is inverted the sum of the two intervals will equal nine. For example, when a second is inverted the new interval is a seventh. The sum of two and seven is nine. Another example: When an interval of a sixth is inverted the new interval is a third. The sum of six and three is nine. This even holds true for unisons. When a unison is inverted the new interval is an octave. The sum of one and eight is nine.

WORKSHEET

1. Identify the following intervals.

Note: When trying to determine an interval where the lower note is not that of a practical keynote, such as D♯, omit the accidental and determine the remaining interval, then replace the sharp or flat and adjust the quality of the interval according to the rules you have learned in this chapter.

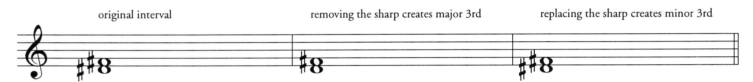

2. Construct the following intervals above the given notes.

INSTRUMENTAL EXERCISES

1. From a variety of arbitrary notes on your instrument play all the major intervals possible. For example, play the note E♭, then play the major second above, then the major third above, the major sixth and the major seventh.

2. From a variety of arbitrary notes play all the minor intervals possible.

3. Play all the perfect intervals you can, then all the diminished and augmented intervals you can. Start from different notes on your instrument.

4. Play any familiar melody on your instrument and determine the interval between each note and the key note.

TRIADS · CHORDS

TRIADS

A *chord* is three or more notes played at the same time. A three-note chord is called a *triad*. All chords are derived from scales. By taking the first, third, and fifth notes from a major scale, we form a major triad.

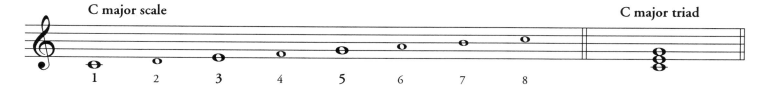

By taking the first, third, and fifth notes from a minor scale, we form a minor triad.

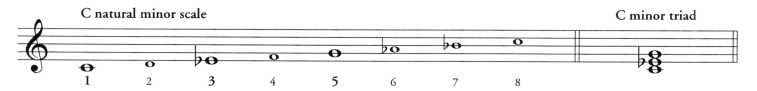

Notice that the major triad and the minor triad consist of intervals of thirds.

The major triad consists of a major third and a minor third.

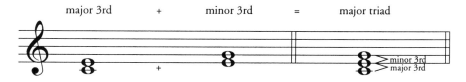

The minor triad consists of a minor third and a major third.

Besides the major and minor triads there are also the augmented and diminished triads.

Augmented triads consist of two major thirds.

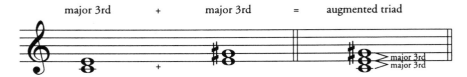

Diminished triads consist of two minor thirds.

After you have learned all of the major triads, it is possible, by following certain formulas, to construct all minor, augmented, and diminished triads.

- To form a minor triad, lower the third of the major triad.
- To form an augmented triad, raise the fifth of the major triad.
- To form a diminished triad, lower the third and fifth of the major triad.

Chords are identified by a *chord symbol,* which is derived from the keynote of the scale from which the chord tones are taken. This keynote is said to be the *root* of the chord. Major chords use just the capital letter and minor chords use the capital letter and a small *m.* Examples: C or Cm. Augmented chords are usually identified by a plus sign (C+) or the abbreviation *aug* (Caug). Diminished chord symbols may feature a degree sign (C°) or the abbreviation *dim* (Cdim).

CHORD INVERSIONS

When the root is the lowest note of a chord, the chord is said to be in *root position.* However, when a chord tone other than the root is the lowest note, the chord is said to be *inverted.*

- When the third of a chord is placed as the lowest note, the chord is said to be in the *first inversion.*
- When the fifth of the chord is placed as the lowest note, the chord is said to be in the *second inversion.*

Notice that although the order of the notes may be changed, the numerical position of each note within the chord is not changed.

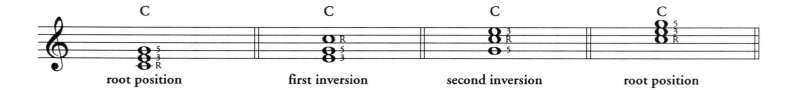

WORKSHEET

1. Identify the following triads by placing the proper chord symbol above each chord. The symbol for an augmented chord is *aug* or +. The symbol for a diminished chord is *dim* or °

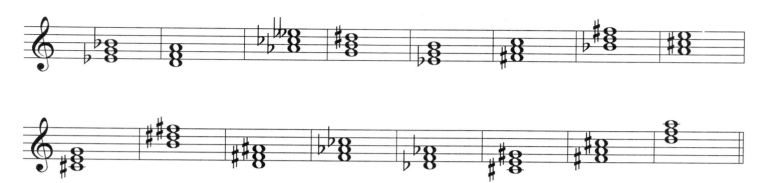

2. Identify the following inverted triads. To find the root of an inverted triad, arrange the triad in successive thirds.

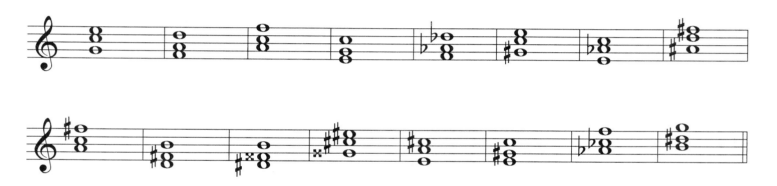

3. Construct triads above the following given notes. The chord symbols indicate the chord quality.

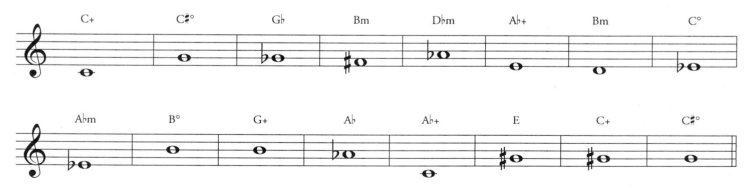

INSTRUMENTAL EXERCISES

1. Using any arbitrary note play a triad above that note. Use that same note as the third and fifth of major, minor, augmented, and diminished triads.

2. Practice singing each of the four basic triads starting from the root, third, and fifth.

MODES OF THE MAJOR SCALE

Within every major scale there are six additional scales called *modes*. Using the C major scale as an example, if we start on the second note of the C scale, D, and play up to the D an octave higher, we have played a *Dorian* mode. It would be the D Dorian mode since it starts on the note D. If we start on the note E and play up to the E an octave higher we have played a *Phrygian* mode. In this case it would be the E Phrygian mode since we started on the note E. If we start on the note F and play up to the F an octave higher we have played a *Lydian* mode. In this case it would be the F Lydian mode. In other words, by starting from each note within any major scale and playing up to the same note an octave higher we have played all the modes contained within that scale. Each note of the major scale becomes a keynote of a new mode. The key signature of each mode is the same as the major scale from which the mode is derived.

Below is the C major scale with all the modes derived from that scale.

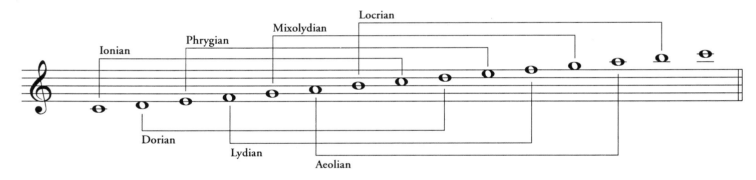

The major scale is also a mode. It is known as the *Ionian* mode.

MODE-RELATED TRIADS

You have learned that the first, third, and fifth notes of the C major scale form the C major triad. By taking the first, third, and fifth notes from each of the six modes within the major scale we form all of the chords that may be used to harmonize any melody based on that particular key. Below is the C major scale and all of its related modes and the chords derived from each.

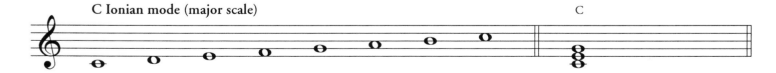

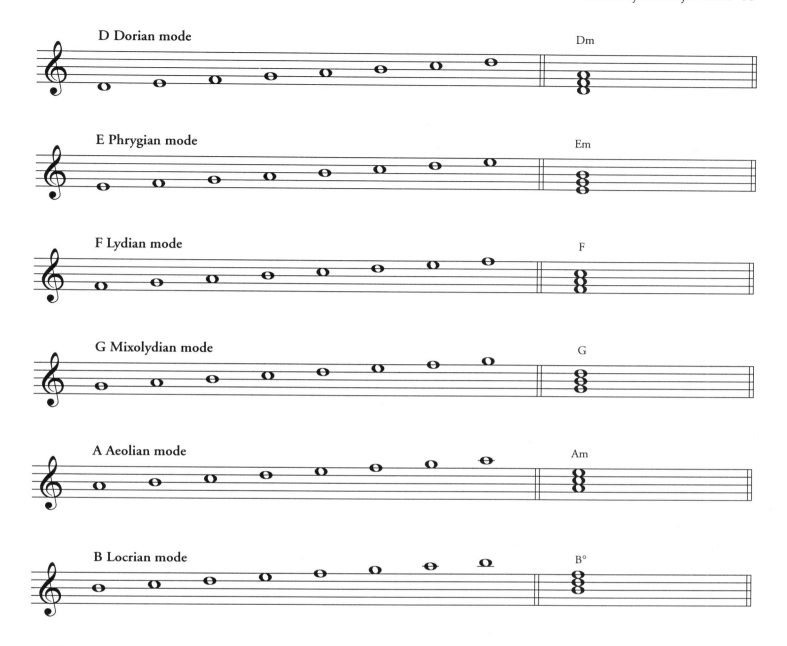

It's important to remember that the key signature of each mode is that of the major scale from which the mode is derived. The key signature of all of the above modes is that of the key of C major: no sharps, no flats.

The following rules should help to better understand how to think of the key signature of any given mode.

- The Dorian mode is formed from the second note of any major scale.
- The Phrygian mode is formed from the third note of any major scale.
- The Lydian mode is formed from the fourth note of any major scale.
- The Mixolydian mode is formed from the fifth note of any major scale.
- The Aeolian mode is formed from the sixth note of any major scale.
- The Locrian mode is formed from the seventh note of any major scale.

Below we see all the different modes formed from the same keynote C. Each mode's key signature will be based on the above rules.

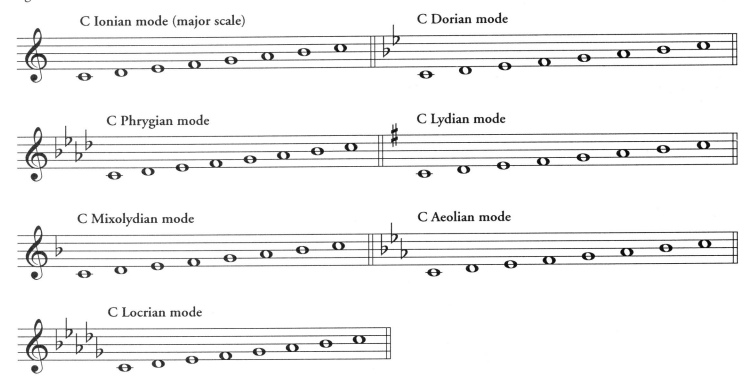

TRIADS OF THE MAJOR SCALE

We just saw how triads are formed from the major scale and all of its related modes. All of the triads formed combine to make up what is known as the *harmonized scale*. That is, all of the triads may be used to harmonize any given melody that is formed by that major scale.

Below we see the C major scale and all of its related triads placed above each note of the scale. Remember that the same principle applies to all major scales.

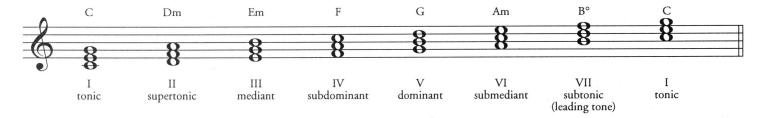

Notice that each triad is identified in three different ways: letter name, Roman numeral, and functional term. The most common way of identifying triads is of course by letter name. Identifying triads by Roman numerals, in which each Roman numeral corresponds to the relative position of the triad in the scale, is also very much favored by musicians. Using Roman numerals makes it possible for a musician to transpose any sequence of chords into any other key. For example, knowing that the progression C Am Dm G is the I VI II V chords means that you can convert those same Roman numerals into any other key; in the key of G, the I VI II V chords would be G Em Am D. Terms such as *mediant* and *supertonic* are not used very often, since they are too cumbersome; however, *tonic* and *dominant* are used quite often.

Note that in all major keys
the I, IV, and V triads are major;
the II, III, and VI triads are minor;
the VII triad is diminished.

Sixth Chords · Seventh Chords

Sixth Chords

A *major sixth chord* is a major triad plus a major sixth above the root.

A *minor sixth chord* is a minor triad plus a major sixth above the root.

A major sixth chord may also be thought of as the first, third, fifth, and sixth notes of the major scale.

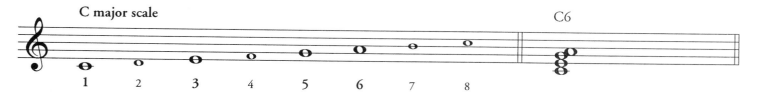

A minor sixth chord may also be thought of as the first, third, fifth and sixth notes of the jazz minor scale.

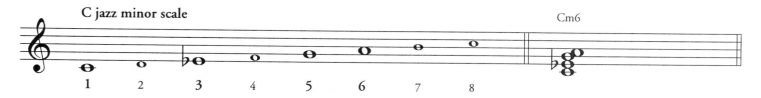

Seventh Chords

Most compositions favored by jazz musicians make greater use of *seventh chords* than triads. A seventh chord is formed by adding a note a third above the triad. There are five different kinds of seventh chords: major seventh, dominant seventh, minor seventh, diminished seventh, and half-diminished seventh. Below we see how each of these different types are formed.

Major Seventh (maj7)

The *major seventh chord* (maj7) chord is formed by adding a major third above the major triad, or by adding a major seventh above the root of a major triad.

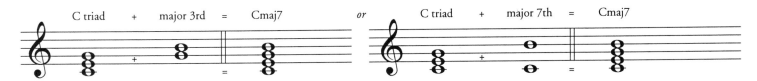

Dominant Seventh (7)

The *dominant seventh chord* (7) is formed by adding a note a minor third above a major triad, or by adding a minor seventh above the root of the major triad.

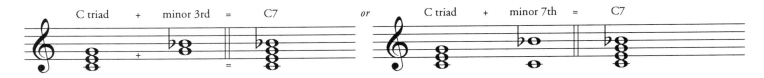

Minor Seventh (m7)

The minor seventh chord (m7) is formed by adding a note a minor third above a minor triad or, by adding a minor seventh above the root of the minor triad.

Diminished Seventh (°7)

A *diminished seventh chord* (°7) is formed by adding a note a minor third above a diminished triad, or by adding a diminished seventh above the root of a diminished triad.

Half Diminished Seventh (ø7)

A *half diminished seventh chord* (ø7) is formed by adding a note a major third above a diminished triad, or by adding a minor seventh above the root of a diminished triad. The chord is often referred to as a *minor seventh flat-five chord* (m7♭5).

INVERSIONS OF SIXTH AND SEVENTH CHORDS

Just as triads may be inverted, sixth chords and seventh chords may also be inverted. When the root of a chord is placed on the bottom, the chord is said to be in *root position;* when the third is placed on the bottom, the chord is said to be in the *first inversion;* when the fifth is placed at the bottom, the chord is said to be in the *second inversion;* and when the sixth or seventh is placed on the bottom, the chord is said to be in the *third inversion*.

Inversions of Sixth Chords

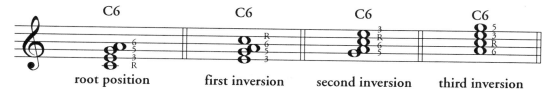

root position   first inversion   second inversion   third inversion

Inversions of Major Seventh Chords

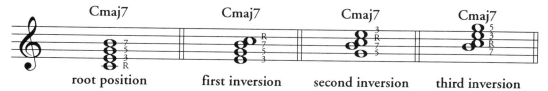

root position   first inversion   second inversion   third inversion

SEVENTH CHORDS AND RELATED MODES

Just as we saw how triads may be formed from the major scale and its related modes, the seventh chords may also be formed in the same way. By taking the first, third, fifth, and seventh notes from the major scale and its related modes, we can form all the seventh chords that may be used to harmonize any melody formed from the major scale.

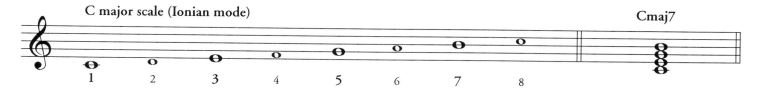

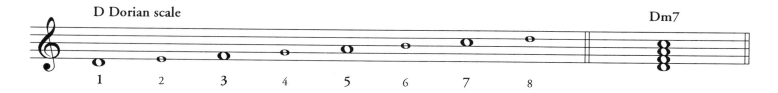

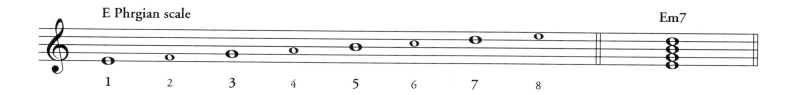

SEVENTH CHORDS AND THE HARMONIZED MAJOR SCALE

By taking all of the seventh chords and placing them over their respective notes within the major scale; we now have the scale harmonized with seventh chords. This is known as the *harmonized scale* or the *diatonic series of seventh chords*. The term *diatonic* refers to the fact that all of the chords consist of notes contained only within that scale.

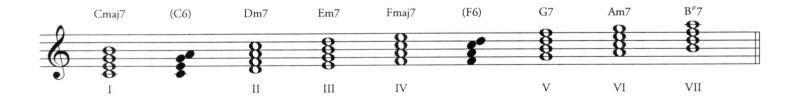

Notice, the I and IV chords are shown as major sixth chords and are often used alternately with the major seventh or in place of the major seventh.

In all major keys:
- The I and IV chords are major seventh (or major sixth) chords.
- The II, III, and VI chords are minor seventh chords.
- The V chord is a dominant seventh chord.
- The VII chord is a half-diminished seventh chord.

CHORD FUNCTION

Before we begin our study of chord progressions, or the manner in which chords move from one to the other, it's important that we know the function of each chord in the diatonic series and the principles governing the movement of chords.

Chord	Function
I	Establishes the key center. Chord of rest. All other chords gravitate toward the I chord.
II	Moves to the V chord (down a fifth). Sometimes acts as a substitute for the IV chord.
III	Acts as a substitute for the I chord. Sometimes progresses to the VI chord.
IV	Used as a temporary new key center. Sometimes acts as a substitute for a II chord and progresses to the V chord.
V	Progresses to the I chord (down a fifth). Creates tension, a sense of movement.
VI	Acts as a substitute for the I chord. Progresses to the II chord (down a fifth).
VII	Acts as a substitute for the V chord. Progresses to the I chord.

Harmonic Movement · The Cycle · Progression · Key Centers

One of the basic principles governing the movement of chords is the fact that there is a strong tendency for a note to move down a perfect fifth (or up a perfect fourth). Notice below, in the C scale, the note G wants to move to the note C; whether down a perfect fifth or up a perfect fourth. Play G followed by the C on your instrument and you will hear this strong pull.

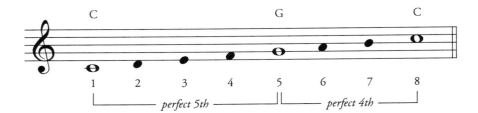

In the same way that G wants to go to C, C wants to go to F, F wants to go to Bb, Bb wants to go to Eb. This principle of notes wanting to move down a perfect fifth has come to be known as moving through the *cycle* (or *circle*) *of fifths* and is often illustrated as shown.

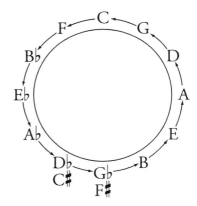

Each letter in the circle represents the root or letter name of a chord. The chords move in the direction shown by the arrows, so that a C chord moves to an F chord, an F chord moves to a Bb chord, a Bb chord to an Eb chord, Eb to Ab, and so on.

The chords represented by the letter names on the circle may all be of the same quality or of mixed qualities. However, great care must be taken so that chords remain within the framework of the diatonic scale. For example. if you want to use the circle to create a progression in the key of C, you must choose chords that have as their roots any of the letters on the circle that go from B to F. If you go beyond the F to the Bb you are out of the key of C. Generally speaking, no more than four chords on the circle are used in any particular key. In the key of C that would be an A chord to a D chord to a G chord to a C chord.

PROGRESSIONS

A *progression* is the movement of one chord to another chord. The smallest possible progression is that of the V chord going to the I chord—the dominant chord to the tonic.

Let's see how progressions are formed within the structure of the major scale. We will use the C scale for our example. The C chord is the tonic. Looking at our circle we see that the root or letter name of the chord that goes to C is G. Below is the C scale with the two chords that form our first progression.

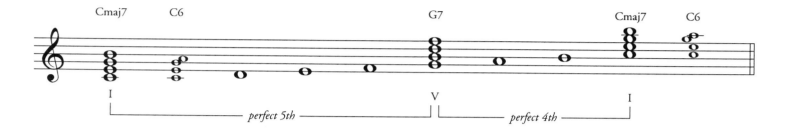

Notice that the G7 chord progresses to the C chord (either C triad, Cmaj7, or C6), thus satisfying the natural urge of the root of the G chord to move a perfect fifth down (or a perfect fourth up) to the root of the C chord. This has come to be referred to as *circular* or *cyclical movement*.

TENSION AND RELEASE

In addition to the principle of circular movement, another reason for the tendency of the V chord to move to the I chord is the principle of *tension and release*. Certain tones in the V chord set up aural tensions that demand resolution to certain rest tones in the I chord. Besides the pull of the root of the V chord to the root of the I chord, the third of the V chord, which is the seventh of the key, also has a strong pull toward the root of the I chord. The fifth of the V chord, which is the second of the key, also wants to move to the root of the I chord. The seventh of the V chord, which is the fourth of the key, wants to move to the third of the I chord. Below is a second inversion G7 (V) chord resolving to the C triad (I). Notice how the arrows show the resolution of the tension tones of the G7 to the rest tones of the C triad.

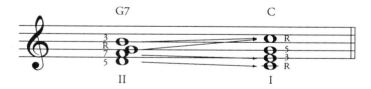

The II V I Progression

One of the most effective ways of creating harmonic interest in a composition is to delay resolution to the I chord. This may be achieved by placing a II chord in front of the V chord. The II chord has certain inherent characteristics that demand movement to the V chord, which in turn demands resolution to the I chord. Delaying resolution is a way of heightening tension, so that when the I chord is finally reached there is a greater sense of release. The II V I progression is one of the most commonly used progressions in popular and jazz music.

Below are several examples of II V I progressions in the key of C. Notice the use of inverted chords which creates a smoother flow from chord to chord.

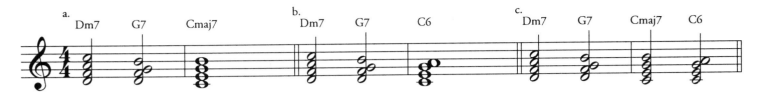

Here are some general rules to follow when moving from chord to chord:

- Keep common tones. In example *a* we see how the root and third of the II chord become the fifth and seventh of the V chord. Also, the root and third of the V chord become the fifth and seventh of the I chord.
- Always move to the next nearest chord tone. In example *a* the fifth and seventh of the V chord move down to the root and third of the I chord.
- Try to connect chord tones in a melodic line. In example *b* the seventh of the II chord (C) moves down to the third of the V chord (B) which in turn moves down to the sixth of the I chord (A). This movement creates a descending melodic line in the top notes of the chords.

The II V I progression is another example of circular movement. The circle of fifths may be used to find the II V I chords in any key. Any letter on the circle may represent the root of a I chord, the letter in front of the I chord; becomes the root of the V chord and the letter in front of that becomes the root of the II. Just remember that the letters around the circle represent the roots of chords of any quality or of mixed quality. For example, let's find the II V I chords in the key of E♭. Here is the circle written out again for convenience.

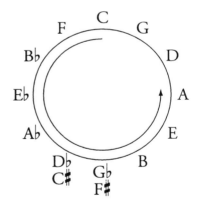

Locating the E♭ on the circle it becomes the root of the I chord, the E♭maj7. The letter in front, B♭, becomes the root of the V chord, the B♭7. The letter in front of the B♭, F, becomes the root of the II chord, the Fm7. So the II V I progression in the key of E♭ is Fm7 B♭7 E♭maj7.

The I VI II V Progression

So far we've seen how the I chord is used to end a progression. Since the I chord is a chord of rest, a chord that establishes the key feeling, it is also often used to start a progression. The progression flows out from the I chord until it finally resolves back to the I after taking many side trips, possibly through a number of other keys. The most commonly found progression beginning with the I chord is the I VI II V progression. Here is the I VI II V progression in the key of E♭.

Chords in root position

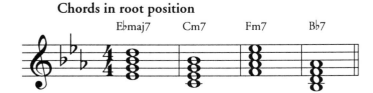

Chords in inverted form

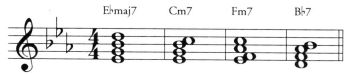

Notice that the VI chord is another link in the circle of fifths. Looking at the circle above, we find the letter C coming before the F. The C represents the root of the Cm7 chord, which is the VI chord in the key of Eb.

Another way of figuring the I VI II V progression in any key is to know the scale of each key and simply count the numbers up on the scale. Remember that the I chord is a major seventh (or sixth), the VI chord is a minor seventh, the II chord is a minor seventh, and the V chord is a dominant seventh chord.

WORKSHEET

1. Write out the II V I progression in the following keys.

KEY	II Chord	V Chord	I Chord
C			
F			
Bb			
Eb			
Ab			
Db/C#			
Gb/F#			
B			
E			
A			
D			
G			

2. Complete in the following sentences.

Dm7 is the VI chord in the key of _____.
B°7 is the VII chord in the key of _____.
C#m7 is the II chord in the key of _____.
F#7 is the V chord in the key of _____.
Dm7 is the III chord in the key of _____.
Cmaj7 is the IV chord in the key of _____.
Bm7 is the III chord in the key of _____.
Abm7 is the II chord in the key of _____.
The VI chord in the key of A is _____.
The III chord in the key of Eb is _____.
The IV chord in the key of Ab is _____.
The IV chord in the key of Bb is _____.
The VII chord in the key of A is _____.
The VI chord in the key of Bb is _____.
The III chord in the key of B is _____.

3. Fill in the missing letters in the circle.

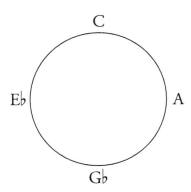

INSTRUMENTAL EXERCISES

1. Using the following as an example, play the diatonic seventh chords in every key.

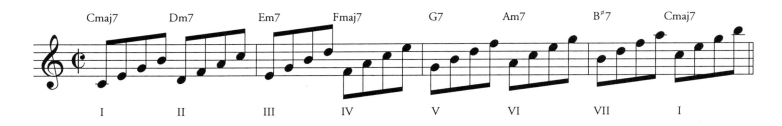

2. Using the following as an example, play the diatonic seventh chords in every key in an alternating down-up pattern.

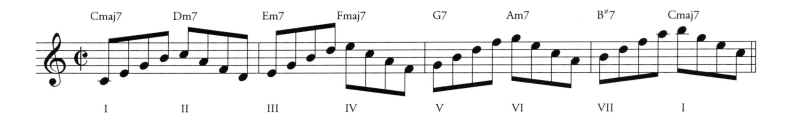

3. Play the II V I progression in every key using the following example.

4. Since the II V progression is found in so many tunes played by jazz players, using the following as an example play through the cycle in the following manner.

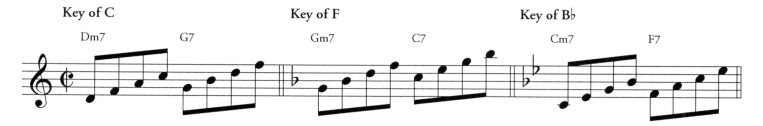

5. Play the II V progression through the circle in the following manner.

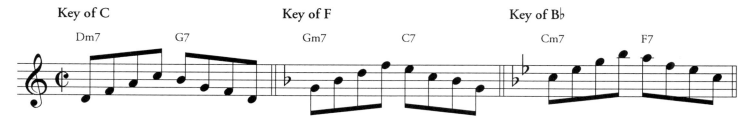

KEY CENTERS

A *key center* refers to a group of notes or chords that create a strong feeling of being in a particular key.

Listen to how the following examples generate a strong sense of the key of C.

Notice how the melody in example *c* strongly suggests the key of C without having to end on the keynote C.

The following examples illustrate the key center of C through the use of chords.

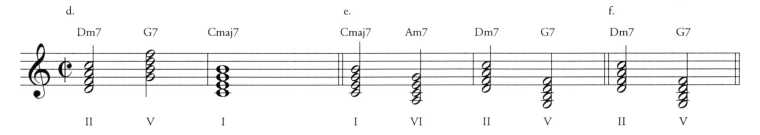

Notice how the chords in examples *e* and *f* strongly suggest the key center of C without having to resolve to the Cmaj7, the I chord. The examples above illustrate how key centers may be indicated by the II V I progression, the I VI II V progression, or the II V progression.

LOCATING KEY CENTERS

Within most musical compositions played by jazz musicians there are often a number of different key centers that occur before the end of the composition. It is particularly important for the jazz musician to be able to recognize these key centers since improvisations are based on the key centers. The following is an example of a composition that might be played by a jazz musician. Notice that the key centers are shown in brackets and that the Roman numeral designations are shown in relation to these key centers.

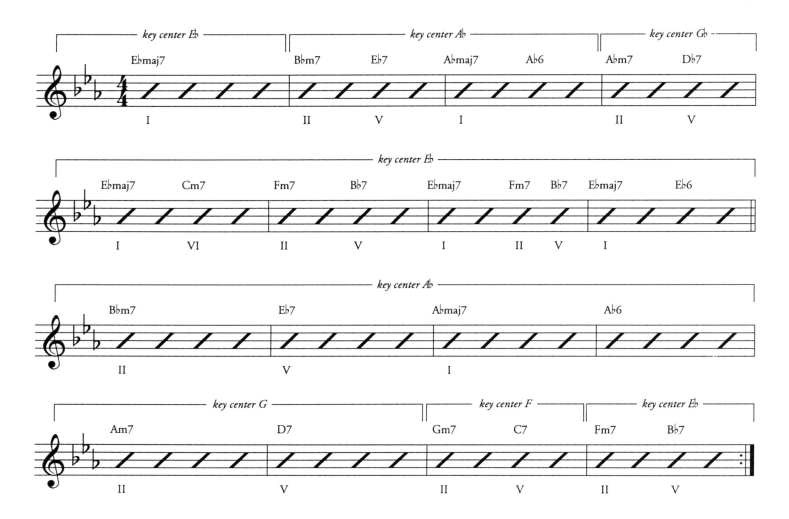

Although the key signature of the above composition is E♭, the progression moves through the keys of A♭, G♭, and F. The progression begins in the first measure in E♭ and in the second measure begins moving into the key of A♭ by playing the II and V chords in the key of A♭. By measure five we are in the key of E♭ again and stay there through measure eight. In measure nine we find the B♭m7 suggesting another II chord; looking ahead, we find the V chord (E♭7) and then its resolution to the A♭maj7, the I chord. From measure thirteen to measure sixteen we see a series of II V chords suggesting the key centers of G, F, and E♭.

Below is another example of a harmonic structure which is very similar to that of the popular song "All The Things You Are." An analysis follows.

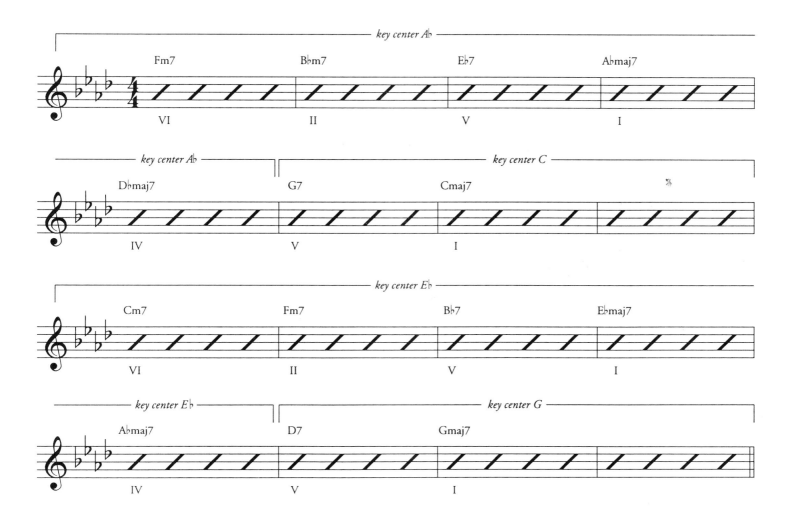

We begin by observing that the key signature is the key of A♭. Looking ahead to the fourth measure, the A♭maj7 chord is the I chord. Looking back to the third measure we know that the E♭7 is the V of the key of A♭; back yet another measure we find the B♭m7, which is the II chord in the key of A♭. Looking now at the first measure we see the Fm7 chord. If we look at our circle of fifths we see that F comes before B♭, making it the VI chord in the key of A♭. Therefore the progression in the first four measures is the VI II V I. In the fifth measure we see D♭maj7. This is the IV chord in the key of A♭. Then, comes G7, which as the V chord establishes the key of C seen in measures six through eight. Measure nine is the beginning of a VI II V I progression in the key of E♭. Measure thirteen is the IV chord in the key of E♭, which moves in measure fourteen to V I in the key center of G.

WORKSHEET

1. Analyze the following harmonic structure as to the key centers. Put in Roman numerals
   to indicate the position of each chord within the key centers.

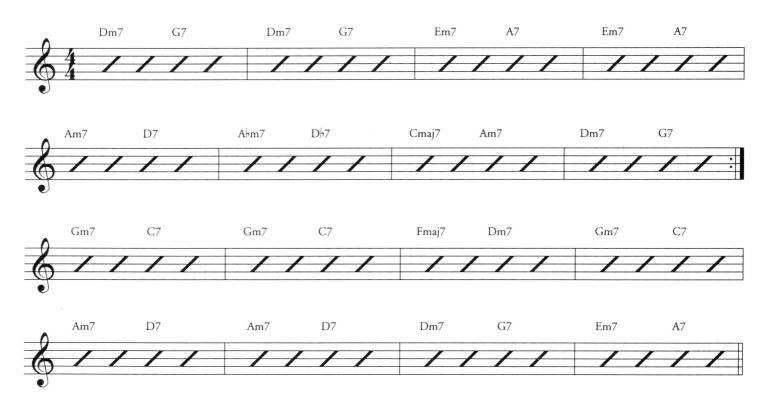

2. Here is another harmonic structure for you to analyze. Put in key centers and Roman
   numerals. The structure is rather unusual, so be careful.

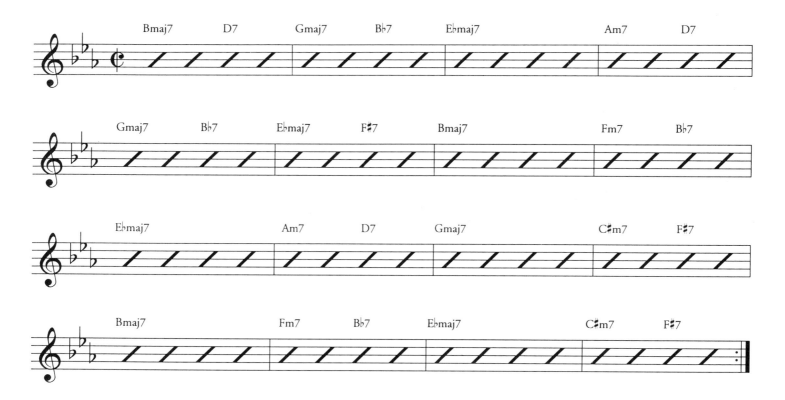

INSTRUMENTAL EXERCISES

The following exercises should be played through the above progressions. Notice that some measures contain two chords while other measures contain one chord. Be sure to play the correct number of counts in each measure.

1. Arpeggiating up each chord.

2. Arpeggiate up one chord and down on the next chord.

3. Playing the first, second, third, and fifth notes of each chord.

4. Going up and down on each chord in irregular patterns. Play the next nearest chord tone and go in any direction you wish.

FORM—THE AMERICAN POP SONG • THE BLUES

The term *form* refers to the structure and design of the various themes used in pop and jazz tunes. An understanding of the different kinds of forms used in this music is very important to anyone who wants to improvise. This knowledge also helps you to memorize tunes and is useful in writing your own compositions.

THE AMERICAN POPULAR SONG FORM—AABA

The most commonly used form in pop and jazz music, the *AABA form,* is sometimes referred to as the "American popular song form" because so many of the great standard tunes fit that form. The form is usually thirty-two bars in length and is usually divided into eight-bar segments or phrases. The first segment is labeled with the letter *A.* Each subsequent segment that has a different theme than *A* will have another letter such as *B,* the next segment with another different theme would be labeled with a letter *C.*

Below, we see how the thirty-two bars are divided into the four segments and labeled. Note that letter *A* is the main theme; since the same theme is repeated in the next segment, it is also labeled *A.* The third eight-bar segment has a different theme, so it is labeled *B.* The final eight bars is a return to the original theme; therefore, it is again letter *A.*

A	A	B	A
main theme	main theme repeated	change of theme	return to main theme

Note that in those tunes that use the AABA form the *B* segment is also referred to as the *bridge* or the *release.* Often a singer might tell the musicians, "I'll sing the first chorus and then I'll skip to the 'bridge.'" The term 'first chorus' refers to the complete AABA form, then the singer will skip right to the letter *B* and finish the song from there. It is important for the musicians to understand this terminology.

Below is a brief listing of some tunes that use the thirty-two-bar AABA form. Try to locate some of these tunes and analyze them as to their structure.

"Blue Moon"   "Heart and Soul"
"These Foolish Things"   "Body and Soul"
"I Got Rhythm"   "Honeysuckle Rose"
"Misty"   "Somewhere over the Rainbow"
"Satin Doll"   "I'm in the Mood for Love"

Not all AABA tunes are thirty-two bars in length. For example, the tune "Yesterday" by Paul McCartney is an AABA tune, but the *A* segments are seven bars each and the *B* segment is eight bars. Another Beatles tune is Lennon and McCartney's "And I Love Her." The *A* segments are ten bars in length and the *B* segment is eight bars in length. The popular bossa nova "The Girl from Ipanema" has eight-bar *A* segments, but the *B* segment is sixteen bars in length. Another popular tune is "My Secret Love," which has sixteen-bar *A* segments and an eight-bar *B* segment.

Sometimes the normal thirty-two-bar AABA form is doubled, making it a sixty-four-bar form with each segment receiving sixteen bars. An example of that form is the standard tune "I Get a Kick out of You." Another tune is the one that is very popular with the beboppers, "Cherokee." It is sixty-four bars in length and each segment has sixteen bars. Another variation on the thirty-two-bar form is to cut it in half and have a sixteen-bar form with each segment receiving four bars. Some examples of that are "Summertime," "Doxy" by Sonny Rollins, and another popular tune from the 1930s "Pretty Baby."

More Form Variations

In addition to the basic thirty-two-bar AABA form and its variants there are many variations in terms of added segments and bars of unusual lengths. Here are some well-known songs with unusual forms. Remember that each segment that has a different letter has a different melody.

"Something": A (nine) A (ten) B (eight) A (nine) A (twelve); a total of fifty-six bars.
"I'll Remember April": A (sixteen) B (sixteen) A (sixteen); a total of forty-eight bars.
"Cheek to Cheek": A (sixteen) B (sixteen) C (sixteen) D (sixteen) E (sixteen); a total of seventy-two bars.
"Begin the Beguine": A (sixteen) B (sixteen) C (sixteen) D (sixteen) E (sixteen) F (twelve) G (sixteen); a total of 108 bars.

Worksheet

Below are some examples of tunes containing other lettered segments. Locate these tunes and analyze them in terms of the numbers of bars in each segment.

ABAC
"How High the Moon"
"Here's That Rainy Day"
"Laura"
"Our Love Is Here to Stay"
"Love Walked In"

ABCD
"My Funny Valentine"
"Stella by Starlight"
"Somebody Loves Me"
"Tonight"
"April in Paris"

The Blues

The other form that occupies such a large part of every jazz musician's repertoire is the *blues*. The blues is a twelve-measure form, but unlike the American popular song form, the blues does contain a definite basic chord progression. All blues compositions must have the I, IV, and V chords placed at certain strategic points within the twelve-measure structure.

Basic Blues Form

Although the I and IV chords are major sevenths, quite often when playing the blues the I and IV chords are played as dominant seventh chords.

There are many variations on the blues progression; we will see some of them shortly.

Just as the popular song form is divided into sections, the blues song form is also divided into sections. The twelve measures are divided into three sections of four measures each and may be labeled AAB.

Below is a blues song form with lyrics.

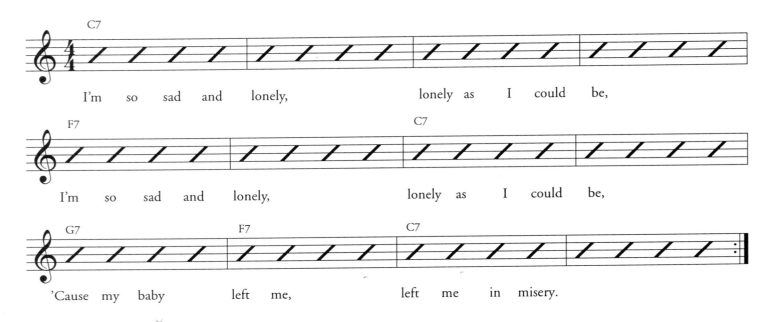

Notice how the second *A* line is simply a repeat of the first *A* line and the *B* line is an answer to the two *A* lines.

There are a number of songs that have the word "blues" or "blue" in the title but are not really blues, since they do not conform to the blues form of twelve measures and do not use the I IV V chord progression. These songs use the word "blues" to describe the mood of the song. One example of such a song is "The Birth of the Blues," which uses the thirty-two-bar AABA form.

There are some eight and sixteen measure tunes that jazz musicians accept as blues tunes because they do make use of the I IV V chords and have a feeling of the blues. One of these blues is "Watermelon Man" by Herbie Hancock; it is a sixteen measure blues.

The blues progression has gone through many changes since it was first heard in the early 1920s with its basic progression as shown above. In the 1940s the musicians of the bop period added a great many chords to the basic progression. Then in the 1950s with the popularity of rhythm and blues, and in the 1960s, with the explosion of rock and roll, the blues went back to its simple, basic progression. We will explore these different blues progressions later in this book.

Since the 1920s the blues form has been heard in thousands of tunes played by jazz, rhythm and blues, and rock players. Here is a brief listing of some of the more commonly heard blues compositions.

"Dippermouth Blues"	"Stormy Monday"
"West End Blues"	"Good Rockin' Tonight"
"One O'Clock Jump"	"Shake, Rattle and Roll"
"In the Mood (Main Theme)"	"Rock around the Clock"
"Bag's Groove"	"Can't Buy Me Love"
"Billie's Bounce"	"Opus de Funk"

Just looking at the very brief listing of blues tunes above we see that the blues progression was used by jazz players of every era beginning with New Orleans jazz ("Dippermouth Blues," "West End Blues") to the swing era ("One O'Clock Jump," "In The Mood"). In the bebop era, blues progressions made up a large part of the repertoire of jazz players ("Bag's Groove," "Billie's Bounce"). The rhythm and blues era of the late forties used mostly blues progressions ("Stormy Monday Blues," "Good Rockin' Tonight"). Following rhythm and blues came rock and roll based largely on the blues ("Shake, Rattle and Roll," "Rock around the Clock"). Even the Beatles used the blues form and chords with "Can't Buy Me Love." In the funky period the blues again played a big role ("Opus de Funk").

As stated earlier, the blues progression lends itself to many variations. Below are several examples of blues progressions.

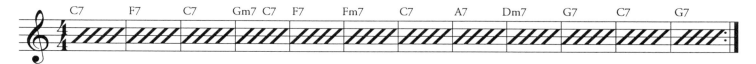

Notice that in the following variation of the blues the I and IV chords are played as major seventh chords. In the sixth measure the IV chord is played as a minor seventh.

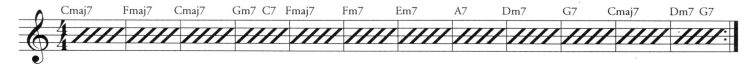

This next variation is often called "Bird's Blues" since it was used by Charlie Parker. It will be explained in greater detail later in the book.

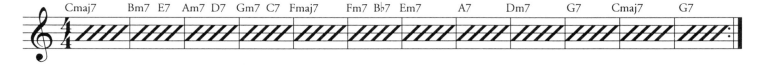

WORKSHEET

1. Choose several records and listen to each one to try to figure out the form of the song. It may take many listenings to each record in order to determine the form, but keep at it. Decide if it is an AABA form, an AAB song, an ABAC form, etc. Then decide how many measures are in each section. This will help your powers of concentration.

2. Using the blues on page 54 as a model, write your own blues choruses (lyrics). After you have worked out your blues lyrics try fitting the words over the blues chord progressions.

3. Choose several printed songs, either from collections of songs or single sheets, and analyze them for form.

4. Answer the following questions.

   How many measures in two choruses of blues? _____
   How many beats are in two choruses of blues? _____
   How many measures are in two choruses of "Misty"? _____
   How many beats are in two choruses of "Somewhere over the Rainbow"? _____

INTRUMENTAL EXERCISES

1. Take each of the three blues progressions on page 55 and play arpeggios through each one. First start each chord from its root and then mix up the notes any way that sounds good to your ear. Use the exercises on page 51 as a guide.

REHARMONIZATION · EMBELLISHING CHORDS · FILL-IN CHORDS · CHORD SUBSTITUTION

Reharmonization is a term used to describe the process of strengthening or revising a weak progression in order to create more interest or to add more color to the progression. There are a number of devices or techniques we can use in this process.

EMBELLISHING CHORDS

An *embellishing chord* is a chord used to prepare, or precede, another chord. The embellishing chord is not part of the original progression, but is added to it. It is sometimes referred to as a *fill-in chord* because it fills in space when an original chord is being held too long and is said to be *static,* or not moving.

Below we see a progression of two measures of a V chord followed by its I chord. Two measures of any chord would create a static or nonmoving progression. To strengthen the progression we can use a II chord to prepare the V chord. See the various examples below.

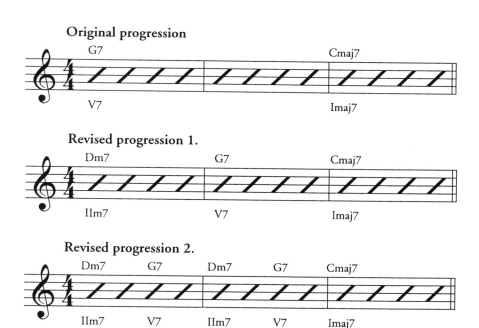

The same V I progression may also be played for one measure.

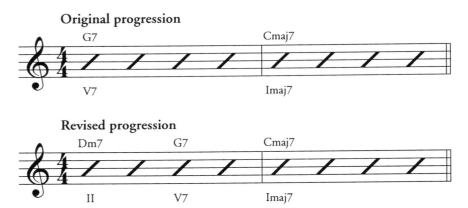

Original progression

G7   Cmaj7

V7   Imaj7

Revised progression

Dm7   G7   Cmaj7

II   V7   Imaj7

A good rule of thumb to follow in the use of the embellishing chord is that any V7 chord may be preceded (embellished) by its IIm7 chord. (You may want to review the section "The II V I Progression" on page 43.)

FILL-IN CHORDS

Another way to create interest in a rather static, or harmonically deficient, progression is to use fill-in chords. For example, when a I chord is played for two measures you may fill in chords by using the IIm7 and the IIIm7 chords of the harmonized scale. This device is best used when the melody is not very elaborate and is best when the melody is stationary.

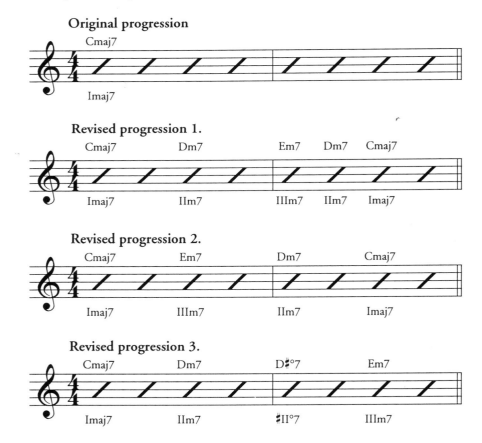

Original progression

Cmaj7

Imaj7

Revised progression 1.

Cmaj7   Dm7   Em7   Dm7   Cmaj7

Imaj7   IIm7   IIIm7   IIm7   Imaj7

Revised progression 2.

Cmaj7   Em7   Dm7   Cmaj7

Imaj7   IIIm7   IIm7   Imaj7

Revised progression 3.

Cmaj7   Dm7   D♯°7   Em7

Imaj7   IIm7   ♯II°7   IIIm7

Notice in the revised progression 3, the D♯ diminished seventh chord is used as a connecting chord between the Dm7 and the Em7 chords. Notice also the Em7 on the third and fourth beats of the second measure. The Em7 is the III chord in the key of C, the III chord is often used in place of the I chord because of the number of common tones between the two chords.

Below is another example of a progression strengthened by the use of fill-in chords.

Original progression

Revised progression

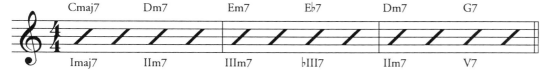

Notice that in the above example the E♭7 chord in the second measure of the revised progression functions as a chromatic embellishing chord to the Dm7 in the third measure. The Dm7 chord in the third measure is the embellishing chord of the G7 and sets up a II V progression.

BACKCYCLING

Backcycling is just another away of using fill-in chords to create more harmonic movement in a static harmonic progression. The word *backcycling* refers to the concept of working backwards through the cycle to find the fill-in chords.

Below are the first five measures of a basic blues progression in the key of B♭. Our task is to create a better movement from the B♭maj7 to the E♭maj7.

Since we are moving to the E♭maj7 chord that chord, becomes our "goal" chord. Let's think of the E♭maj7 as a temporary I chord. Looking back to the cycle we see that the letter name of the chord before the E♭ is B♭. We can use a B♭7 chord going to our E♭maj7 to make a V I progression. Notice that in front of the B♭ is the letter F; therefore we can put some kind of F chord in front of the B♭7. The chord that comes before a dominant seventh is a minor seventh, so we will put an Fm7 in front of the B♭7, making a II V progression.

Continuing to backcycle, we now think of the Fm7 as a temporary I chord. Once again looking at the cycle, we find that we can put a C7 in front of the Fm7. Backcycling farther we can now put a Gm7 in front of the C7, creating another II V I progression.

Now think of the Gm7 as a temporary I chord; looking at the cycle we see that we can put a D7 in front of the Gm7 and an Am7 in front of that. Our final progression is seen below. (Note that this progression is the same as the beginning of "Bird's Blues," which you played earlier.)

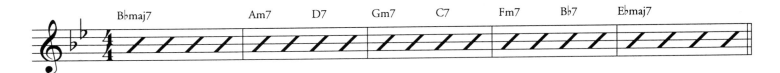

To understand the concept of backcycling, it is important to remember that we are working backwards around the cycle from whatever chord we choose as our goal chord. Treat that goal chord as a temporary I, put a V7 chord in front of it and a IIm7 chord in front of the V7. Continue this process as far as it is needed and as far as it sounds good. Be sure there is no conflict with whatever melody is being played over the progression.

CHORD SUBSTITUTION

A *chord substitution* refers to the replacement of one chord with another chord. The new chord will have a new root or letter name. Another kind of substitute chord is one that has the same letter name but a different chord type. For example, A7 would be a substitute chord for Am7.

Common-Tone Substitution

One chord may replace another chord when the substitute chord and the original chord have two or more common tones. To better understand this, look at the harmonized scale once again.

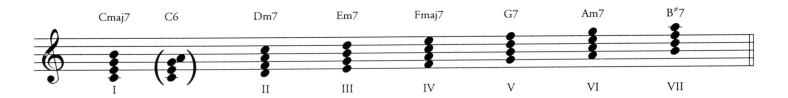

Notice below that the I chord, the Cmaj7, contains three tones that are also in the III chord, the Em7.

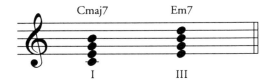

Notice also that the notes contained in the C6 chord are exactly the same as the notes in the VI chord, the Am7.

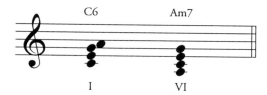

We can conclude from the above that either the III chord or the VI chord may be used as a substitute for the I chord.

An example of the use of chord substitution is shown below. The original progression is a turnaround, a I VI II V progression. The substitute chords create a sequence of II V progressions.

Original progression

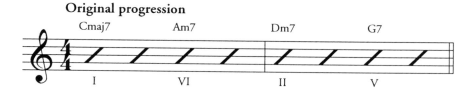

Substitute progression

The Em7 is a substitute for the Cmaj7 based on the common-tone rule, III for I. The A7 is a substitute for the Am7 based on the rule that one chord may substitute for another chord of the same letter name if the quality of the chord is different.

Other examples of chord substitutions based on common tones are shown below.

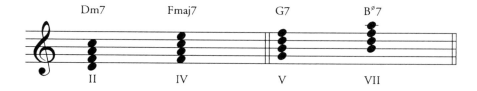

We can conclude from the above that the IV chord is a substitute for the II chord and that the VII chord may substitute for the V chord.

Flat-Five Substitution (Tritone Substitution)

The *flat-five substitution* is a device usually applied to the dominant seventh chord and occasionally the minor seventh chord. The substitute chord is a dominant seventh built on the flatted fifth of the original chord. For example, in a G7 chord the fifth is the note D. The substitute chord would therefore be a D♭7. The D♭ is the flatted fifth of the G7 chord. The two most important notes of any chord are the third and seventh; both of these two notes are in the original chord and the substitute chord. This is another example of substitution by common tones.

Notice that the B (third) and the F (seventh) of the G7 become the seventh and third of the D♭7 chord. (The C♭ is the enharmonic equivalent of the B.)

The flat-five substitution may also be applied to a minor seventh chord, as in the following examples.

In this first example, we see a II V I progression, Dm7 G7 Cmaj7. Earlier we learned that you may substitute one chord for another chord with the same root or letter name just by changing the chord's quality. Therefore we can substitute the D7 for the Dm7, then use a flat-five substitution for the D7.

Original progression

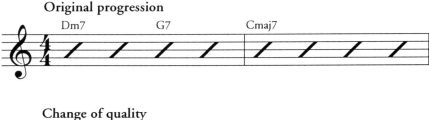

Change of quality

♭5 substitution

Another example of substituting for a minor seventh is in the I VI II V progression. Using the same principle as above we arrive at the following substitution.

Original progression

Change of quality

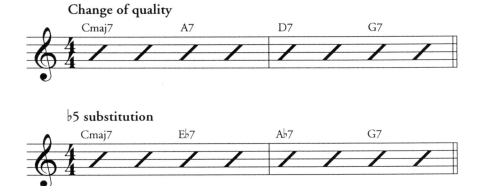

♭5 substitution

By using the III chord substitution for the I and the flat-five substitution for the VI and the V chord, we arrive at the following substitute progression for the I VI II V progression. It creates an interesting descending chromatic bassline.

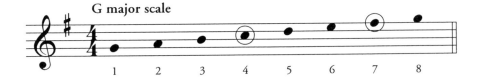

The most important rule to follow when using any chord substitution is to avoid any conflict with the melody. The above example of a substitution for the I VI II V progression is in the turnaround where the melody is usually a held note, so the substitution provides some harmonic interest.

THE TRITONE

The principle behind the flat-five substitution is the *tritone*. The tritone is an interval of two notes that are three whole tones, or whole steps, apart. For example, the notes in a D7 chord are D, F♯, A, and C. The tritone is F♯ to C. The flat-five substitution for D7 is A♭7, made up of A♭, C, E♭, and G♭. Note that the C to G♭ (F♯) is the same tritone as in the D7 chord. The third and seventh of the D7 chord become the seventh and third of the A♭7 chord. These two notes are the *tension notes* of two scales, the G scale and the D♭ scale. The scales are shown below with the tension notes circled.

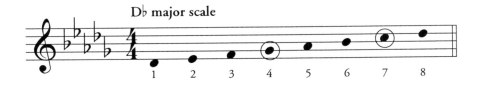

Tension notes always want to resolve to rest notes. The *rest notes* are the tonic and third notes of the scale. Below we see how the tritone of the D7 chord (F♯ and C) resolves to the rest tones of the G chord, creating the V to I progression.

All dominant seventh chords may move down a perfect fifth.

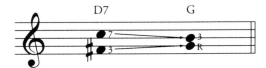

Now we see how the tritone of the A♭7 chord (C and G♭) also resolves to the G chord. Notice that the notes of the tritone are inverted to create a smoother move into the G chord.

All dominant seventh chords may move down a half step.

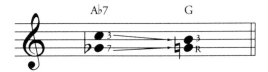

Here flat-five substitute chord moves to the I chord, resolving down half step, from A♭7 to G.

Just as the A♭7 chord is the flat-five substitution for the D7 chord, the D7 chord is the flat-five substitution for the A♭7 chord.

A♭7 is the V chord in the key of D♭. Looking at the D♭ scale we find that it contains the tension notes that make up the tritone of the A♭7 chord and the D7 chord (the F♯ in the D7 is the enharmonic equivalent of G♭). Therefore, the A♭7 chord resolves to the D♭ chord because of the V I progression and the D7 chord also resolves to the D♭ chord because all dominant seventh chords may resolve a half step down.

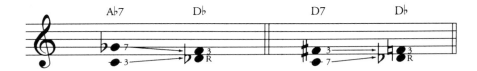

Another variation on the flat-five substitution is to use it together with its original chord.

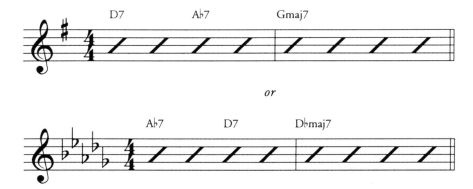

In summary, we can conclude that all dominant seventh chords may resolve to the I chord either by cycle motion—V to I (G7 to Cmaj7)—or by the half-step down approach—(D♭7 to Cmaj7).

Extended Chords · Altered Chords · Approach Chords

Ninth Chords

All seventh chords may be extended to ninth chords by adding a note a major ninth above the root. (The major ninth is the same letter name as the major second but an octave higher.) Below are examples of various ninth chords. Notice that ninths may also be added to the major sixth chord, the diminished seventh chord, and the half-diminished seventh chord.

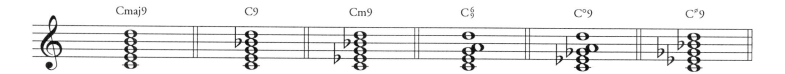

When adding a major ninth to a minor seventh chord be sure the minor seventh is not functioning as a III chord, as in a diatonic progression such as Cmaj7 Dm7 Em7. In this situation adding a major ninth to the Em7 chord would give you an F♯ which obviously is not in the key of C. This rule also applies to the half-diminished seventh chord when it is functioning as a VII chord. The added major ninth would not be in the key of the I chord.

Eleventh Chords

All ninth chords may be extended to eleventh chords by adding a note a third above the ninth. However in popular and jazz music the eleventh must be treated according to current practices; for example, when adding the eleventh to major ninth, major sixth/ninth, or dominant ninth chords, the eleventh should be a major third above the ninth. When adding the eleventh to a minor ninth chord, the eleventh should be a minor third above the ninth. as in the examples below.

Note that there is much confusion in the notating of certain chord symbols. For example, the major eleventh chord is sometimes notated as maj9aug11, or maj11, or maj9add♯11. The minor eleventh chord is sometimes written as m9add11, or m11. When using the sharped eleventh in a chord, the fifth of the chord is sometimes omitted to avoid a clash.

THIRTEENTH CHORDS

The thirteenth may be added to most of the chords shown above. The thirteenth is the same letter-name as the sixth and is a major interval. Below are examples of different kinds of thirteenth chords. Note the alternate chord symbols.

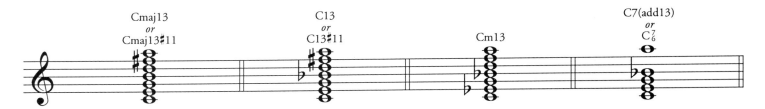

Note that the C7(add 13) does not contain a ninth or an eleventh. It is very important to understand that the ninth, eleventh, and thirteenth chord tones are all optional and may be included or omitted in any combination. For example, you may have a C7 chord and indicate that you want to add just the eleventh (♯11) without the ninth included, or you may want the C7 with just the thirteenth (sixth) and no ninth or eleventh as shown above. Also, when you are given a chord symbol which indicates a ninth, eleventh, and thirteenth it is your prerogative whether to use any of those added chord tones. The function of the chord remains the same whether you use the added tones or not. A C13 has exactly the same function as a C7. The added tones only produce a fuller, more dissonant sound, creating greater tension.

Conversely, if a C7 is indicated you may play any or all of the possible added tones, the ninth, eleventh, or thirteenth. The choice is strictly personal and should depend on the style of the music being played. For example, when playing in the style of pop-rock, simpler chords such as triads and seventh chords are best used. For jazz styles of greater complexity, it would be more appropriate to use added chord tones such as ninths, elevenths, and thirteenths. The more acquainted you are with all of the various music styles the better you will be able to make a choice.

If you play a chording instrument, it is also important to know which chord tones may be omitted in order to be able to finger these larger chords. It isn't necessary to play every note in a chord. The root of a chord may be omitted, as can be the fifth of a chord. Only the third and seventh must be included in every chord since these are the color tones. The third tells whether the chord is major or minor, and the seventh is an important color tone and is always used except in the case of a §chord. The seventh also helps to establish the function of a chord. For example, in a C7 chord the seventh, B♭, establishes that the chord is a dominant chord. In a Cmaj7, the seventh—although it sounds a bit dissonant—does establish that the chord is a tonic chord.

ALTERED CHORDS

An *altered chord* is any chord that contains one or more notes that are not in the key or scale from which the chord is derived. For example, a C7♭5 chord contains the notes C, E, G♭, and B♭. The C7 chord is the V chord in the key of F; since there is no G♭ in the key of F, the C7♭5 is called an altered chord. Another example would be a Cmaj7+. The notes are C, E, G♯, and B. The Cmaj7 chord is the I chord in the key of C; since there is no G♯ in the key of C, the Cmaj7+ is considered to be an altered chord. All alterations are indicated in the chord symbols and should present no problem.

Adding extended and altered tones to the chords of any progression can create a richer and more colorful sound. Below is a simple melody based on a II V I progression. The melody is then harmonized a number of ways, beginning with a simple basic harmonization followed by a number of revised harmonizations. Your ear and personal taste will dictate which harmonization you prefer.

Original melody

Original harmonization

Revision 1.

Revision 2.

Revision 3.

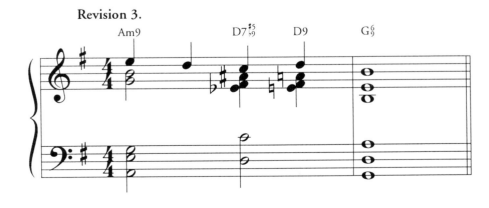

Revision 4.

Another use of altered chords is to accommodate certain notes in a melody. For example, the melody shown below is harmonized with the I VI II V progression. Notice, however, that some of the notes of the melody are not part of the basic chords; therefore, alterations have to be made in the chords. The E♭ in the first measure is not part of the Am7 chord, so the chord is altered to accommodate the E♭, making the chord an Am7♭5. The A♭ in the second measure is not part of the G7 chord, so the chord has to be altered to accommodate the A♭. The resulting altered chord is the G7♭9.

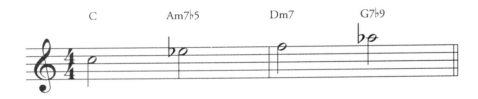

Extended and altered chords may also be used to create harmonic motion against a sustained melody that is harmonized by a single chord. For example, below we see a melody note G held for four counts and harmonized by a G7 chord. The melody note may either be played or sung by another musician. Instead of simply holding the G7 chord for a whole measure, resulting in a rather lifeless accompaniment, altered chords may be used to create a feeling of activity or motion, generating greater interest.

Original harmonized melody

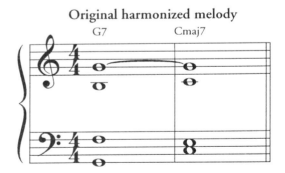

Melody with revised harmonization

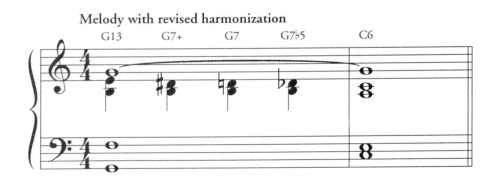

Notice in the revised harmonization of the G7 chord, we now have a descending melodic line played in the top voice of each new chord, thus creating some feeling of movement while the melody note G is sustained.

Below is an example of how the basic blues progression may be reharmonized by the addition of extended, altered, and substitute chords. An analysis will follow.

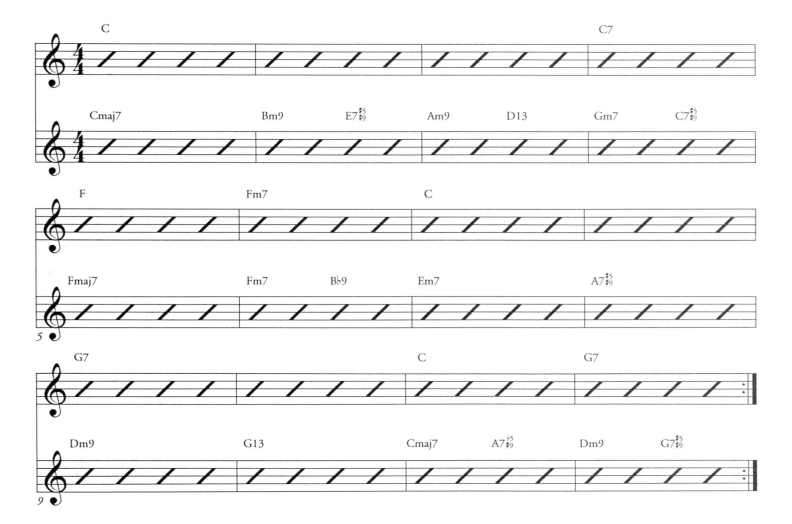

Measure 1: The first measure of the blues is basically a I chord. Most traditional blues players play the I chord as a dominant seventh, while more modern players may use a major seventh. I chose a major seventh in the reharmonization.

Measures 2, 3, and 4: In order to create harmonic movement in these measures, I have chosen to use some fill-in chords based on the principle of backcycling.

Measure 5: The IV chord may be played as either a dominant seventh or a major seventh.

Measure 6: Here the major seventh is changed to a minor seventh setting up a II V situation.

Measure 7: The Em7 is a substitution for the original C chord. (The III chord is a substitute for I.)

Measure 8: The A7$^{\sharp5}_{\sharp9}$ is an altered chord arrived at by backcycling from the Dm9.

Measure 9: The Dm9 is an extended II chord and is an embellishing chord of the G13.

Measure 10: The G13 is an extended G7 chord.

Measures 11 and 12: The progression in the last two measures is referred to as a *turnaround* Turnarounds are discussed in the next chapter.

APPROACH CHORDS

All chords may be preceded by a chord either a half step above or a half step below. This new chord is called an *approach chord* and is generally of the same type as the chord it precedes. Below is a part of a progression used very often by jazz players and found in hundreds of popular standard tunes of the 1930s and 1940s.

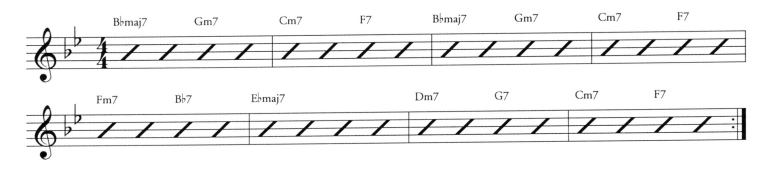

Below is the same progression shown above but with added approach chords. Note also that the Gm7 chord in the first measure is now played as a G7 chord.

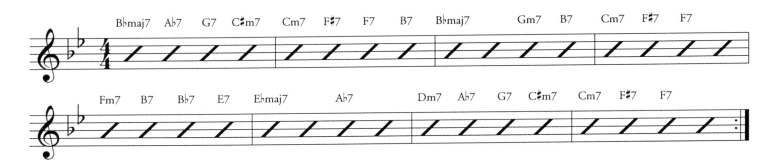

Below is a progression based on a series of II V chords.

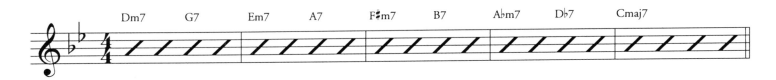

Below is the same progression shown above with added approach chords.

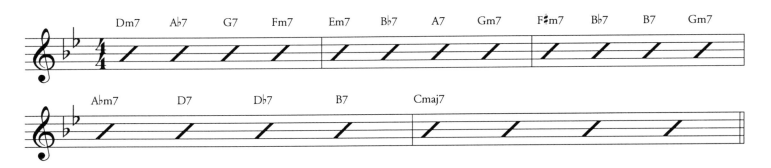

WORKSHEET

1. Below is the eighth measure of the first *A* section of an AABA tune. The chord in the first measure of the tune is also Gmaj7. Fill in a chord on each of the remaining three beats of the eighth measure.

2. Add some fill-in chords to make the following progression more interesting.

3. Use approach chords to make the following progressions more interesting.

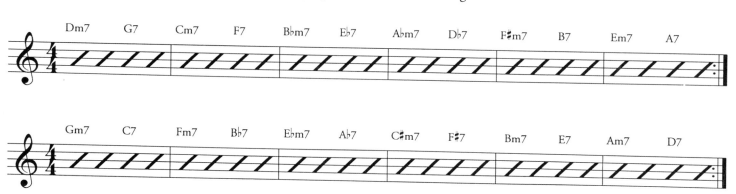

INTRODUCTIONS · ENDINGS · TURNAROUNDS

INTRODUCTIONS

Another use of the backcycling process is in the playing of introductions to songs. If you are a keyboard player or guitarist, you are sometimes called upon to play an introduction to a song. The introduction has to be so constructed that the last chord leads smoothly and musically into the first chord of the song. For example, if the first chord of the song is a Imaj7, that chord is our "goal" chord. We then work backwards. We know that the last chord of the introduction should be the V7 chord leading to that I chord. We can then put a II chord before the V chord. In order to lengthen our introduction we can then think of that II chord as another goal chord, or temporary I, and put another V chord in front of that. This process can continue as far back as you need depending on how long the introduction should be.

Below is an example of backcycling from the starting chord of a song in order to create an introduction to that song.

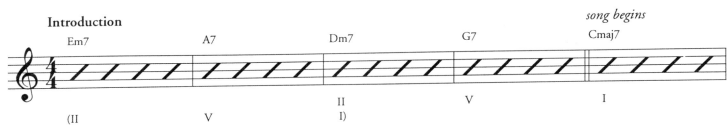

Below is another, simpler example of backcycling from the goal chord, the first chord of the song.

The following example illustrates how an introduction to a song that begins on a II chord (such as "Satin Doll") may be created by backcycling.

Below is a simpler example of an introduction to a song beginning on a II chord.

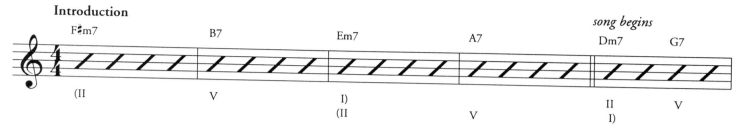

ENDINGS

Ending a song is another opportunity to use your imagination. A song usually ends on a I chord, the tonic chord, with the melody usually ending on a sustained chord-tone. As the accompanist, you want to create some harmonic interest behind that note. Below are several possibilities.

In this first example, the sustained note (melody note) is the third of the key. After playing the I chord on the first beat the harmony skips up to the IV chord and then descends diatonically, or scalewise down to the I chord again.

In the above example you are accompanying a singer or another instrumentalist. But there are times when you are playing the melody on either piano or guitar and, when ending the song, you may want to sustain the last note (in this case the third of the key). In that situation you could voice the chords shown above so that the melody note is always heard in the top voice, or the top note.

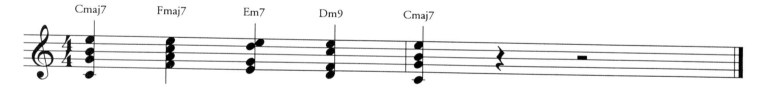

In this next example the melody note could be either the root or the fifth of the I chord. Start the ending on the I chord and then go through the cycle alternating major sevenths and dominant sevenths until you reach the chord a half step up from the final I chord.

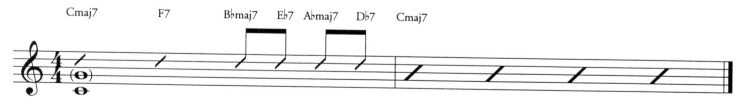

In this next example of a possible ending, the melody note is the fifth of the I chord. This ending works best when the first chord of the ending is a I chord. Instead of playing the I chord substitute a III chord and then descend chromatically alternating between minor sevenths and dominant sevenths.

In this ending the fifth is again the melody note. The ending starts with the III chord descending a half step down, then goes through the cycle leading to the chord a half step above the I chord and ending on the I chord.

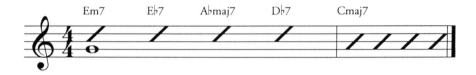

In this last example we begin on the IV chord and descend chromatically using all major seventh chords. In order to play the chords watch out for the syncopated figure on the third beat, first measure.

Some of these endings may also be used as introductions when the first chord of the song is a I chord. The final chord of a song is also a I chord, so the goal is the same—to move to the I chord. The only difference is that in the ending you are playing against a melody and you have to be aware of any clash between the chords and the melody.

TURNAROUNDS

The *turnaround* is a chord progression occupying one or two measures at the end of a section of music while preparing for a repeat of that section. One example of the use of the turnaround is in the eleventh and twelfth measures of the blues progression, since the blues is often repeated a number of times. Below are the last two measures of the blues progression in the key of C.

Since the blues progression begins on the I chord in measure one, the turnaround should be a chord or a sequence of chords that provide for a return to the I chord. Such a sequence of chords is the I VI II V progression shown below.

Turnaround

The above progression should be used each time the blues progression is repeated. On the last chorus of the blues omit the turnaround and end on the normal I chord.

Another place where the turnaround may be found is in the seventh and/or eighth measures of the first or third *A* section of the standard AABA American pop song form. Below is an example of the chords as might be seen in the eighth measure of the AABA song form; then we see the turnaround.

Original eighth measure

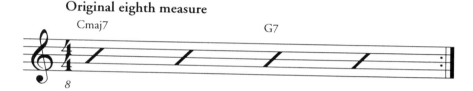

Eighth measure with turnaround

As with any progression, substitutions may be used to create more harmonic interest. In the case of the turnaround, the movement back to the I chord may be made smoother with the use of the following series of substitute chords. Note that the Em7 is a substitution for the Cmaj7 (III for I), the Eb7 is a substitution for the Am7 (flat-five substitution), and the Db7 is a substitution for the G7 (flat-five substitution).

Original turnaround

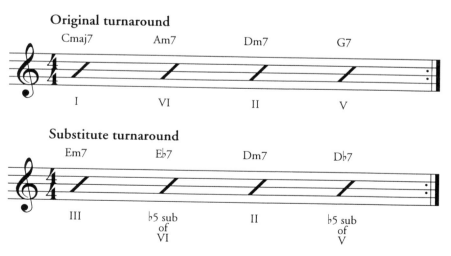

In a turnaround, the most important thing to remember is that you are returning to the first chord of the tune. Any series of chords that does that should work, provided there is no conflict with the melody. Generally, there is not much melodic movement in the measures that contain the turnaround. If the first chord in the first measure of the tune is a II chord, then follow the same principles found in the section on introductions.

Below is another example of a turnaround in a tune that has a I chord in the first measure.

WORKSHEET

1. Write in the ♭5 substitution for the following chords.

E♭7 _____	F♯7 _____
B♭7 _____	C♯7 _____
D♭7 _____	B7 _____
G♭7 _____	E7 _____
A7 _____	F7 _____

2. Which two chords contain the following tritones?

E and B♭ _____	F and C♭ _____
A and E♭ _____	G and D♭ _____
G♯ and D _____	A♯ and E _____
D♯ and A _____	E♯ and B _____

3. Write out the notes to the following chords.

C7$^{b5}_{\sharp9}$ _____   Ab$^{6}_{9}$ _____

B7$^{\sharp5}_{b9}$ _____   Db7$^{b5}_{b9}$ _____

Bb7$^{b9}_{\sharp9}$ _____   Eb13$^{b9}_{\sharp11}$ _____

F$\sharp$13 _____   A13 _____

Db9$\sharp$11 _____   E7(add$\sharp$11) _____

4. Write a chord introduction to the following "goal" chords.

Introduction

Introduction

Instrumental Excercise

1. Arpeggiate through the revised blues progression shown on page 69.

Harmonic minor scale · Jazz minor scale

The Harmonic Minor Scale and Its Related Modes and Seventh Chords

Just as we learned that within every major scale there are six additional scales called modes, we will now learn about the harmonic minor scales and the modes related to those scales. For our example we will use the C harmonic minor scale. Remember that the harmonic minor scale is formed by raising by a half step the seventh note of the natural minor scale, and that the natural minor scale is built from the sixth note of its relative major scale. Therefore, the C harmonic minor scale is formed by raising the seventh note of the C natural minor scale, which is the relative minor of E♭ major. That is the reason why the key signature of C harmonic minor contains three flats. Notice also that the modes are not named as in the major scale—Dorian, Phrygian, *etc.,*—but are numbered according to their position within the harmonic minor scale. Notice too that the chords are formed by taking the first, third, fifth, and seventh notes from each mode.

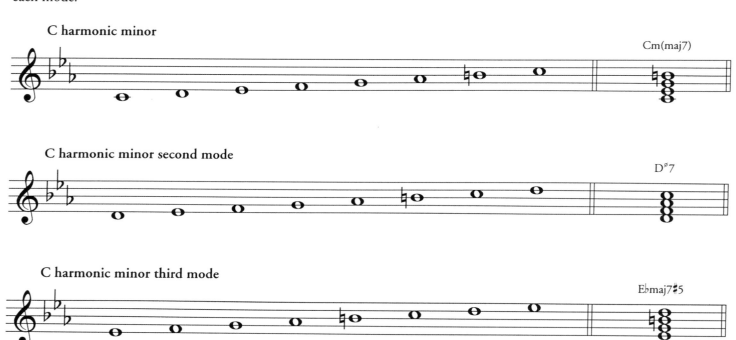

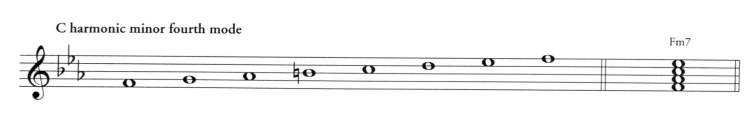

C harmonic minor fifth mode

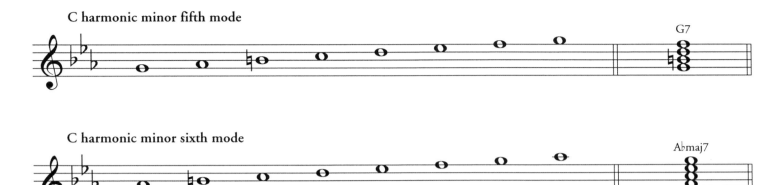

C harmonic minor sixth mode

C harmonic minor seventh mode

THE HARMONIZED HARMONIC MINOR SCALE

By placing all of the chords derived from the harmonic minor scale and its related modes over each note of the harmonic minor scale, we have what is referred to as the *harmonized harmonic minor scale.*

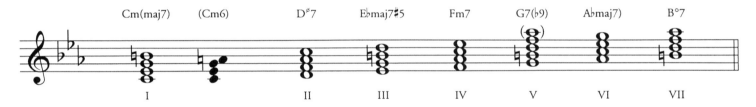

Notice that the alternate I chord, the Cm6, contains a raised, or in this case a natural, sixth (A♮) even though this is inconsistent with the scale. (The sixth note of the C harmonic minor scale is A♭.) The minor sixth chord is formed by adding a major sixth over a minor triad. That construction is the rule regardless of the scale. If the scale contains a flatted sixth then theoretically the chord symbol could rightfully contain a natural placed next to the 6, but in common practice that is omitted (Cm6 instead of Cm♮6.)

Notice also that the V chord is extended to include the ♭9 the V7♭9 is more definitive than the V7 chord in the harmonic minor scale. Here the A♭ is maintained, unlike in the minor sixth chord.

THE II V I PROGRESSION IN MINOR

As in the major keys, the II V I chord progression establishes a key feeling. This progression should be memorized in every minor key. Below we see the progression in the key of C minor.

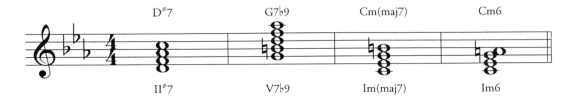

Note that the I chord may be either or both forms of the chord, the Im(maj7) or Im6.

The Jazz Minor Scale and Its Related Modes

The jazz minor scale is the ascending portion of the melodic minor scale. It may be conceived of as the natural minor scale with raised sixth and seventh steps. Or, it may be best, and more simply, thought of as the major scale with the third lowered. That is how we will think of the jazz minor scale. This scale with its related modes is very useful in a variety of improvising situations; you would be well advised to learn them. Below is the C jazz minor scale and its related modes. Notice that no chords are shown as in previous scale chord studies. The chords related to the jazz minor scale will be explained more adequately in the section "The Harmonized Jazz Minor Scale."

C jazz minor scale

D Dorian ♭2 scale

E♭ Lydian augmented scale

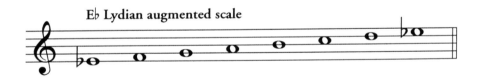

F Lydian ♭7 scale

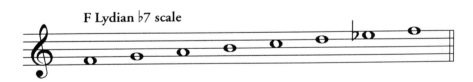

G Mixolydian ♭6

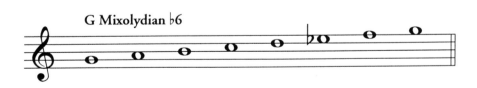

A Locrian ♯2 scale

B super Locrian scale

MODES OF THE JAZZ MINOR SCALE PLAYED FROM THE SAME ROOT

Below are some of the most commonly used modes derived from the jazz minor scale. All are played from the same root. We will see at least two ways in which each mode may be derived.

As we learned earlier, the jazz minor scale may be thought of as the major scale with the lowered third. Another way to think of the jazz minor scale is as the natural minor scale with the sixth and seventh raised.

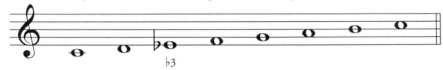

C jazz minor scale (compared to C major)

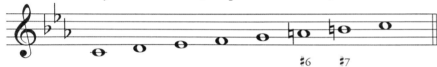

C jazz minor scale (compared to C minor)

Lydian Augmented
This is the third mode of the jazz minor scale; it may be thought of as the major scale with a raised fourth and fifth. It may also be thought of as the Lydian mode of the major scale with the raised fifth.

C Lydian augmented scale (compared to C major)

C Lydian augmented scale (compared to C Lydian)

Lydian ♭7

This is the fourth mode of the jazz minor scale. It may be thought of as the major scale with a raised fourth and a lowered seventh, or the Mixolydian mode with a raised fourth, or also as a Lydian with a lowered seventh.

C Lydian ♭7 scale (compared to C major)

C Lydian ♭7 scale (compared to C Mixolydian)

C Lydian ♭7 scale (compared to C Lydian)

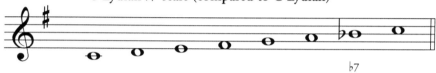

Locrian ♯2

This mode is the sixth mode of the jazz minor scale. It may be thought of as a major scale with a lowered third, fifth, sixth, and seventh, or as the Locrian mode with a raised second.

C Locrian ♯2 scale (compared to C major)

C Locrian ♯2 scale (compared to C Locrian)

Super Locrian

This is the seventh mode of the melodic minor scale. It may be thought of as a major scale with a lowered second, third, fourth, fifth, sixth, and seventh, or as the Locrian mode with a lowered fourth.

C super Locrian scale (compared to C major)

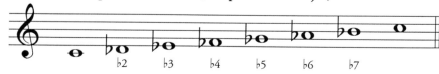

C super Locrian scale (compared to C Locrian)

Creating Modes from Any Root Tone

Another way of creating the modes from any root tone is to relate the mode to the particular jazz minor scale from which the mode is derived. For example, the Lydian augmented mode is built from the third note of the jazz minor scale. C Lydian augmented is the third mode of the A jazz minor scale, and contains the same notes as that scale. In order to find the jazz minor scale relative to the Lydian augmented mode, simply go back a minor third from the root of the Lydian augmented.

C Lydian augmented scale

A jazz minor scale

The Lydian ♭7 mode contains the same notes as the jazz minor scale built a perfect fourth lower. For example, C Lydian ♭7 contains the same notes as the G jazz minor scale, beacause G is a perfect fourth below C.

C Lydian ♭7 scale

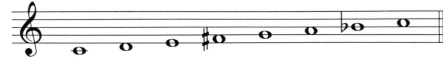

G jazz minor scale

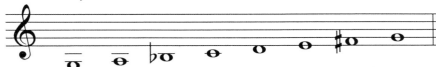

The Locrian ♯2 mode contains the same notes as the jazz minor scale built a minor third higher. For example, C Locrian ♯2 contains the same notes as the E♭ jazz minor scale, because E♭ is a minor third above C.

C Locrian ♯2 scale

E♭ jazz minor scale

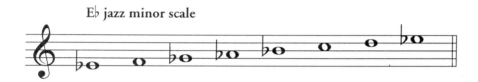

The super Locrian mode contains the same notes as the jazz minor scale built a half step higher. For example, C super Locrian contains the same notes as the D♭ jazz minor scale. D♭ is a half step higher than C.

C super Locrian scale

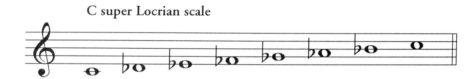

D♭ jazz minor scale

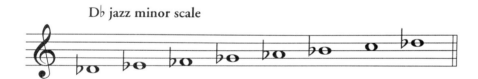

It is important to remember that when creating the mode, you start from the root of the mode but use the same notes as its related jazz minor scale. However, when improvising it might be just as easy to think of the jazz minor scale. For example, if you are improvising over a chord that uses the G super Locrian mode you can improvise on the A♭ jazz minor scale. Since G is the seventh degress of the A♭ jazz minor scale, this will produce the G super Locrian mode.

WORKSHEET

The jazz minor scale is such an important scale for the jazz improviser that it is essential that you have a thorough understanding and command of that scale. Remember that it is the major scale with the third lowered. Construct jazz minor scales on the following root tones.

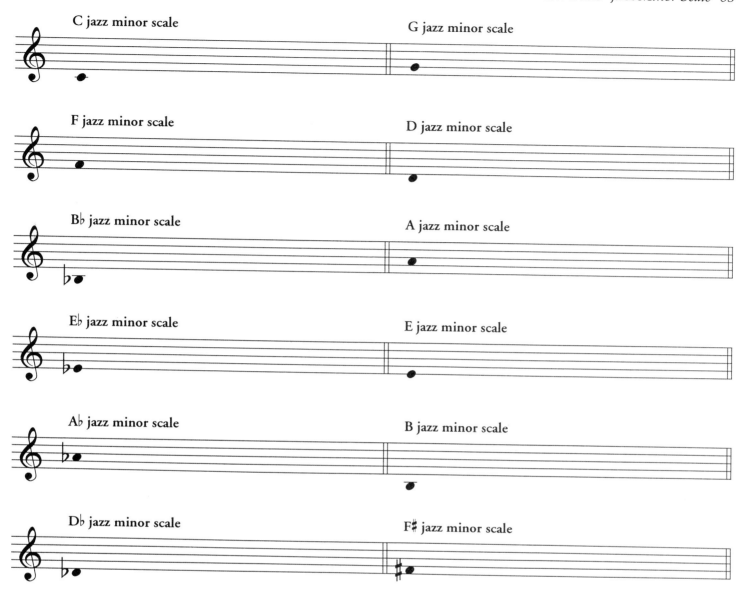

All of the above jazz minor scales should be memorized and played on your instrument in every octave using a variety of patterns.

THE HARMONIZED JAZZ MINOR SCALE

Traditionally, the harmonized minor scale shown at the beginning of this chapter has been used to harmonize tunes played in minor keys. However, one of the most commonly used progressions, I VI II V, cannot be harmonized by the chords of the harmonic minor scale because it contains a ♭VI chord which destroys the bass line. Therefore, jazz and pop musicians have developed a harmonized minor scale that works well with that progression.

This new harmonized minor scale is a combination of the harmonic minor and the jazz minor scales. The jazz minor scale provides the roots of the chords while the harmonic minor scale provides the notes that are built over the jazz minor scale.

C harmonic minor scale

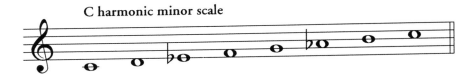

C jazz minor scale

Harmonized C minor scale

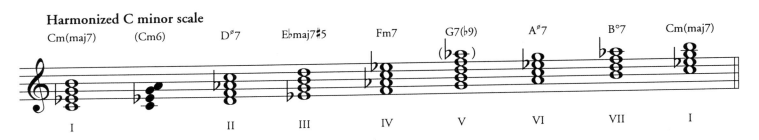

Note that the alternate I chord is a Cm6. This is explained under the section on the harmonized harmonic minor scale, as is the V7 chord's extension to the ♭9.

Essentially, the only difference between the harmonized harmonic minor scale and the above harmonized scale is the VI chord.

MINOR-KEY CHORD PROGRESSIONS

Just as in major keys, the two most commonly found progressions in minor are the II V I progression (as discussed in the last chapter) and the I VI II V progression shown below. This progression could not be played with chords derived solely from the harmonic minor scale because of the lowered VI chord, however, with the harmonization of the jazz minor scale, the progression can now be played.

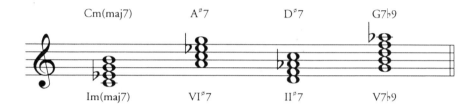

Note that when playing in the minor key the V chord is usually shown as a 7♭9 chord, since the ♭9 is a distinguishing and definitive sound of the minor key.

THE Im Im(maj7) Im7 Im6 PROGRESSION

The Im Im(maj7) Im7 Im6 progression is found in many major tunes that move into a temporary minor key feeling. The chords are derived from a combination of several scales. The Im, Im(maj7), and Im6 chords may be derived from either the harmonized harmonic minor scale or the jazz minor scale; the Im7 chord is derived from the Dorian mode. What makes this progression so interesting is the descending melodic line that connects each of the chords. The line may be played as the top note of each chord, or it may be played as the bassline.

moving line in top voice

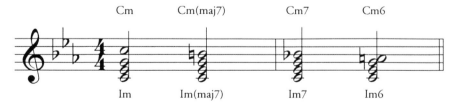

moving line in bottom voice

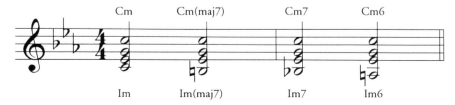

When a minor chord is given for one or two measures, the Im Im(maj7) Im7 Im6 progression may be used to create greater harmonic interest.

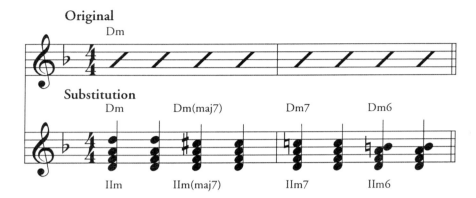

Notice the descending melodic line in the top voice of the revised progression. This progression is more interesting than just holding the basic minor chord.

The Im Im(maj7) Im7 Im6 progression may also be used in place of a II V progression, since the IIm6 chord is in fact a V9 chord without the root.

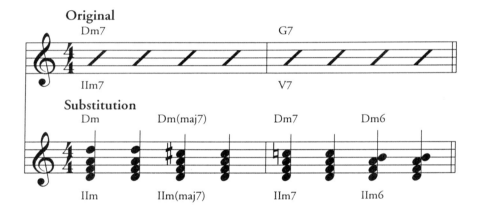

Blues in Minor

The following progression is just one of many variations of the blues progression as played in minor.

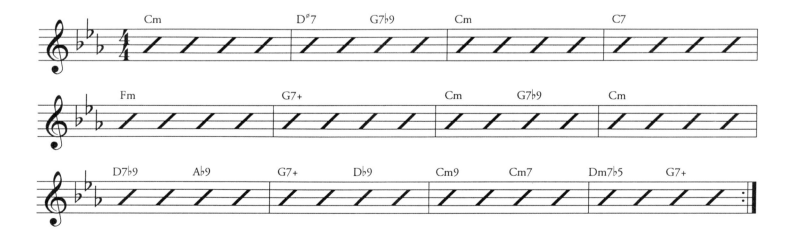

SUBSTITUTION FOR THE MINOR SIXTH CHORD

The minor sixth chord functions as a Im6 chord in a minor key. It also plays an important function in creating minor melodic moving lines. In these situations it is not desirable to replace the minor sixth chord. However, there are situations where the minor sixth chord simply does not contribute much to a progression and should be replaced. Below we will see two examples of when a minor sixth could be replaced with another chord.

1. When a minor sixth chord is followed by a dominant seventh whose root is a whole step higher than the root of the minor sixth, replace the original minor sixth chord with a minor seven flat-five chord whose root is the fifth of the dominant seventh chord. Below are several examples.

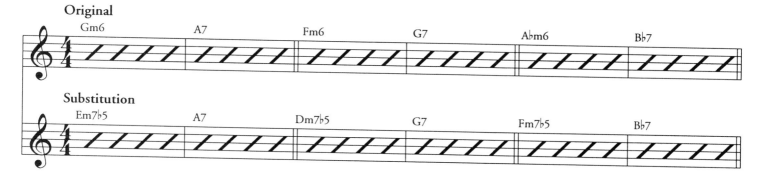

Notice that although the substitute chord is just an inversion of the original chord, the new root provides better bass line movement because it sets up the cyclical movement of the II V sequence.

2. Another example where a minor sixth chord may be replaced is when it is followed by a major seventh chord whose root is the fifth of the minor sixth, as in a IVm6 Imaj7 progression. The minor sixth may be replaced by a dominant ninth chord whose root is a perfect fifth down from the root of the original chord. Below are several examples.

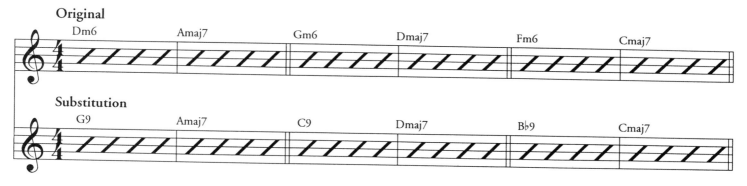

DIMINISHED SEVENTH CHORDS · AUGMENTED CHORDS · SUSPENSIONS

DIMINISHED SEVENTH CHORDS

The diminished seventh chord is a very interesting and useful chord. Its special relationship to the dominant seventh flat-nine chord makes the diminished seventh chord a natural substitute for the dominant seventh chord. Let's see what the relationship is.

Below are four dominant seventh flat-nine chords.

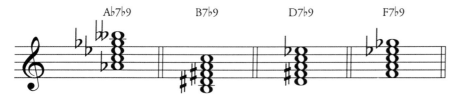

If we omit the root from each of the above dominant seventh flat-nine chords the remaining notes form diminished seventh chords.

Note that each diminished seventh chord is constructed of equal minor third intervals; therefore, any of the notes within each chord may be considered the root of the chord.

If you look carefully at each of the above chords you will notice that each chord contains exactly the same notes (observe the enharmonic notations: F♯=G♭, D♯=E♭, A=B♭♭). From this we can conclude that C°7, D♯°7(E♭°7), F♯°7(G♭°7), and A°7 are all the same chord because they all contain the same notes.

Below are four more dominant seventh flat-nine chords and their related diminished sevenths. Notice that C#°7 (Db°7), E°7, G°7, and A#°7 (Bb°7) may all be considered to be inversions of the same chord.

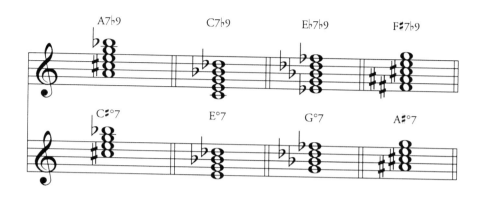

Here are the final four dominant seventh flat-nine chords and their related diminished seventh chords.

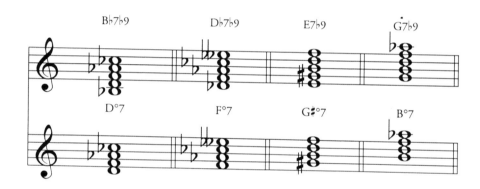

We can conclude from the above that D°7, F°7, G#°7 (Ab°7), and B°7 are all the same chord.

In summary, we can say that there are three different diminished seventh chords, with each chord having four possible names (plus their enharmonic equivalents).

The diminished seventh chord is generally used to connect two chords, either ascending or descending. Below are several examples.

The diminished seventh is used to connect the I chord to the II chord.

This is an extension of the above progression.

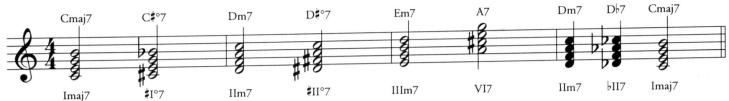

Here the diminished seventh is used to connect a IV chord to the V chord using a descending bass line.

We just learned that the root of a diminished seventh chord is the third of a dominant seventh flat-nine chord. Therefore, a good substitution for a diminished seventh chord would be a dominant seventh chord or a dominant seventh flat-nine chord. For example, for a C°7 chord we may use an A♭7 or an A♭7♭9 chord. The A♭ is a third below the C, the root of the C°7 chord. To take this one step further we can place an E♭m7 chord in front of the A♭7. The reason for this is that all dominant seventh chords may be preceded by the IIm7 chord. We can conclude by saying that every diminished seventh chord may be replaced by a II V progression.

Below we see the II V substitution for every diminished seventh chord.

Original Diminished Seventh Chord	IIm7	V7
C°7	E♭m7	A♭7
E♭°7	F♯m7	B7
G♭°7 or F♯°7	Am7	D7
A°7	Cm7	F7
C♯°7	Em7	A7
E°7	Gm7	C7
G°7	B♭m7	E♭7
B♭°7	D♭m7	G♭7
D°7	Fm7	B♭7
F°7	A♭m7	D♭7
A♭°7	Bm7	E7
B°7	Dm7	G7

Because every diminished seventh chord has four possible names, each chord has four possible II V substitutions. For example, an A°7 may be replaced by either Cm7 F7, Am7 D7, F♯m7 B7, or E♭m7 A♭7. Although theoretically any of the II V progressions should work, your ear should tell you which progression works best. There must be no conflict with the melody.

Below are several examples of diminished seventh chord substitutions.

In the following progression a II V substitution is used for a diminished seventh chord.

Original progression

Substitution

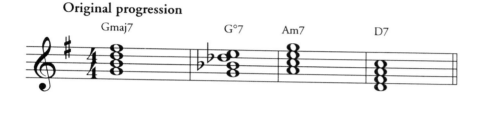

In this next progression we see a III chord substituted for the I chord in the first measure. In the second measure we see a Bb°7 used instead of the given G°7, since any of the notes in a diminished seventh chord may be considered the root. By changing the root we have created a descending chromatic bass line.

Original progression

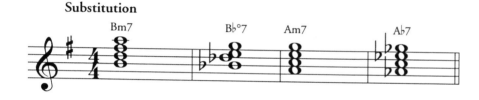

Substitution

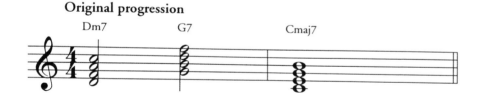

A sequence of diminished seventh chords may be used to replace a II V progression resolving to a I chord. The diminished seventh chords should progress up in minor thirds.

Original progression

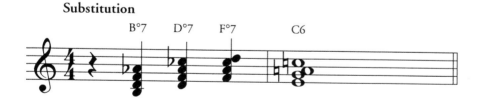

Substitution

Notice that the B°7, the D°7, and the F°7 are all the same chord; only the letter name changes as you progress up in minor thirds. Remember, any of the notes in a diminished seventh chord may be considered the root.

Augmented Chords

In the chapter "Triads • Chords" we learned that an augmented triad is formed from two major third intervals. Another way to construct an augmented triad is to raise the fifth of a major triad, for example, C E G♯. The symbol is either + or *aug*. The augmented triad is generally used in simple harmonic progressions and helps to create a melodic line reinforcing a V I progression.

When you want a stronger chord than an augmented triad, think of the root of the triad as being the seventh of a dominant 9♯11 chord. In the first measure below, the C, root of the C+, becomes the seventh of the D9♯11 chord.

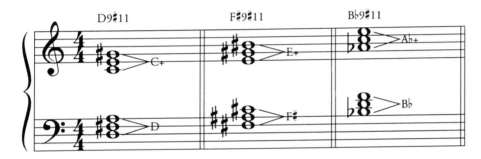

Note that due to the fact that each note in the augmented triad is equidistant from the next, any one of the notes in the triad may be considered the root of the triad.

In summary, we can say that since there are three possible roots to the augmented triad, then there are three possible substitutions for each augmented triad.

Another use of the augmented triad is shown below. This progression is found, for example, in the song "Michelle." The substitution chord is a minor–major seventh chord whose root is the same as the minor chord that precedes it.

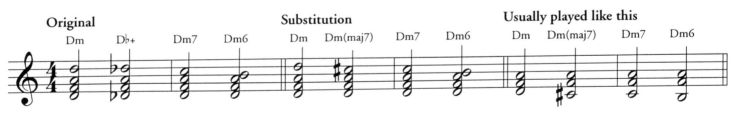

SUSPENSIONS

A *suspended fourth chord* refers to a chord in which the fourth scale step replaces the third of the chord. The suspended note is usually held over from a previous chord. It is used to delay a complete feeling of harmonic satisfaction by holding back an expected chord tone. In the following example, the F in the G7 chord becomes the suspended fourth in the C chord. Note how the suspended fourth resolves down to the expected chord tone E, the third of the chord.

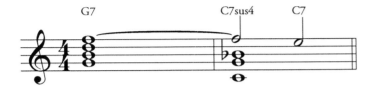

Note how the suspended chord C7sus4 is prepared by the G7 chord. The suspended note is usually a holdover from a previous chord.

Here is another example of a suspension.

Suspended chords are indicated in a number of ways, for example, C7sus4, Csus, C7 with F, Csus4.

A more contemporary method of indicating a suspended chord is by the use of slash marks. For example, if you look back at the C7sus4 above, you will note that the three notes above the C form a Gm7 chord without the fifth. This has led many composers to indicate that chord like this; Gm7/C. Other suspended chord symbols are shown below with their voicings.

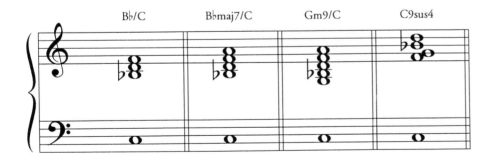

Worksheet

1. Below are a series of augmented triads. Write in the three possible substitutions for each triad.

2. Below are a series of minor sixth chords. Write in the two possible substitutions for each chord.

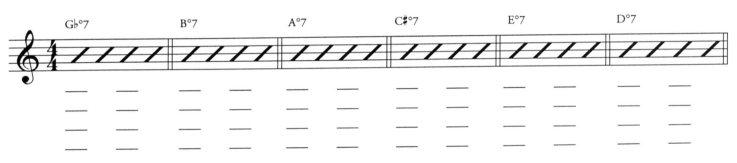

3. Below are a series of diminished seventh chords. Write in the four possible II V substitutions for each chord.

4. In the following exercise there are certain chords that are rather weak and could be improved by substitutions. Write in the chord substitutions you feel would improve the exercise.

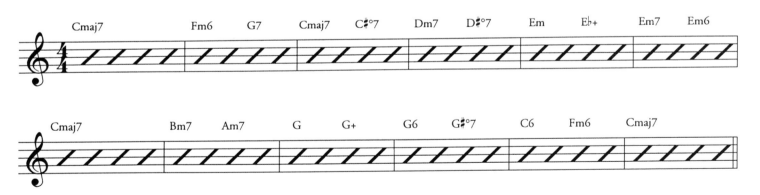

CHORDS AND THEIR IMPROVISING SCALES

Since improvisation plays such a large part in today's pop and jazz music, in this section we will explore some of the possible choices of scales that may be used to improvise over the different kinds of chords.

MAJOR SEVENTH CHORDS

All major seventh chords that function as I chords, and all extensions such as the sixth, ninth, eleventh, and thirteenth are derived from the major scale; so it is that scale that is used to improvise over any of these chords. However, since the fourth of the major scale may sound rather dissonant when played over the major seventh chord, a second choice is the Lydian scale, which provides a raised fourth. Often both the natural fourth and the raised fourth may be used in the same improvised solo.

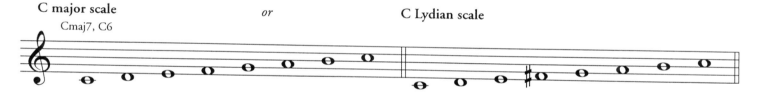

MINOR SEVENTH CHORDS

The minor seventh chord, which functions as a II chord, and all of its extensions are derived from the Dorian mode, so it is that mode which may be used to improvise over that chord.

DOMINANT SEVENTH CHORDS

The dominant seventh chord is derived from the Mixolydian mode, so the scale of choice for improvising over the dominant seventh chord and all of its extensions—the ninth, eleventh, and thirteenth—is the Mixolydian mode. The Lydian ♭7 mode may often be preferable because of the dissonance between the third of the dominant seventh chord and the fourth note of the Mixolydian scale. Using the Lydian ♭7 mode eliminates this dissonance. However, it is acceptable to use both the natural eleventh and the raised eleventh in the same improvised solo. If the chord symbol indicates the ♯11 then you must use the Lydian mode.

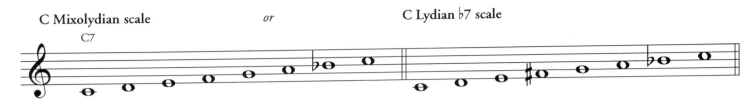

HALF-DIMINISHED SEVENTH CHORDS

The half-diminished seventh chord, also called the minor seventh flat-five chord, is derived from the Locrian mode, and so that mode is the scale generally accepted as the improvising scale for that chord. However, because of a possible conflict between the second note of the Locrian mode and the root of the half-diminished chord, another choice could be the Locrian #2.

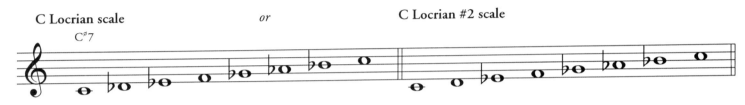

DIMINISHED SEVENTH CHORD · DIMINISHED SCALES

The *diminished scale* is formed by adding a note a whole step up from each note of a diminished seventh chord.

C diminished, E♭ diminished, F♯ diminished, or A diminished scale

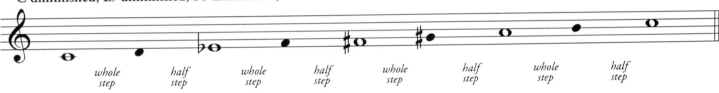

Because of the symmetrical construction of this scale, alternating whole and half steps, any of the notes of the given diminished seventh chord may be considered the letter name of the scale. Therefore, the above scale may be called a C diminished scale, an E♭ diminished scale, an F♯ (G♭) diminished scale, or an A diminished scale.

There are only three diminished scales, each scale having four possible letter names. Below is another diminished scale with four possible letter names.

C♯ diminished, E diminished, G diminished, or B♭ diminished scale

Below is the last diminished scale with its four possible letter names.

D diminished, F diminished, A♭ diminished, or B diminished scale

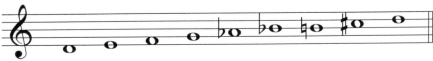

The diminished scale is used to improvise over the diminished seventh chord. The C diminished scale is used to improvise over the C°7 chord.

An even more common use of the diminished scale is in improvising over a dominant seventh chord.

You have learned that every diminished seventh chord is actually a dominant seventh flat-nine chord with the root omitted. For example, a C°7 chord is an Ab7b9 chord without the Ab. Therefore, we can use the C diminished scale to improvise over the Ab7b9 chord. It is also possible, and often happens, that the diminished scale may be used to improvise over the dominant seventh chord even without the b9 indicated in the chord symbol. Let's see what the relationship of the C diminished scale would be to the Ab7 chord.

C diminished scale

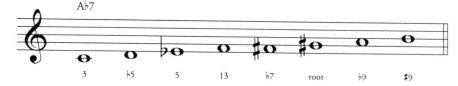

We can see from the above that using the diminished scale over a dominant seventh chord provides such altered notes as the b5, b9, and ♯9. It is these altered notes that create a more colorful and interesting melodic line.

A simple way of deciding which diminished scale to use over a particular dominant seventh chord is to use the scale whose tonic note is a half step higher then the root of the dominant seventh chord. For example, for a G7 chord, use a Ab diminished scale. To go a step further, if we think of the G7 chord as a V chord, we can put the II chord in front of it, making a II V progression, and then use the diminished scale to improvise over the complete II V progression. In other words, the Ab diminished scale may be used to improvise over the Dm7 G7 progression. The table below lists which diminished scales may be used to improvise over any V chord or II V chords.

Diminished Scale	II V Chords
C (Eb, F♯, A)	F♯m7 B7
	Am7 D7
	Cm7 F7
	Ebm7 Ab7
C♯ (E, G, Bb)	Gm7 C7
	Bbm7 Eb7
	C♯m7 F♯7
	Em7 A7
D (F, Ab, B)	Abm7 Db7
	Bm7 E7
	Dm7 G7
	Fm7 Bb7

Another form of the diminished scale is called the *half-step/whole-step diminished scale*. It is formed by adding a note a half step above each diminished seventh chord tone.

C half-step/whole-step diminished scale

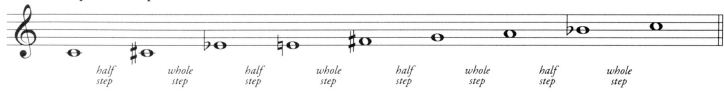

This scale is *not* used over a diminished seventh chord, but it may be used over a dominant seventh chord whose root is the *same* as the letter name of the diminished scale. for example, for a G7 chord you may use the G half-step/whole-step diminished scale.

If you choose to play a diminished seventh chord scale over a dominant seventh chord, be sure to use the correct form of the scale. The half-step/whole-step diminished scale is used with the dominant seventh whose root is the *same* as the letter name of the scale. The whole-step/half-step diminished is used with the dominant seventh chord whose root is a *half step lower* than the letter name of the diminished scale.

ALTERED DOMINANT SEVENTH CHORDS

In the chapter "Extended Chords • Altered Chords • Approach Chords" we learned that chords may be altered to create more interest harmonically or to fit a particular melody. The chord that offers the greatest possibility for altered notes is the dominant seventh. You might see dominant seventh chords with either raised or lowered fifths or raised or lowered ninths or any combination of both. When you have to improvise over any of these altered chords it is important that the improvising scale contain those altered notes.

Dominant Seventh Flat-Five or Augmented Chords

A dominant seventh chord with either the lowered fifth or raised fifth or both may use a scale called the *whole-tone scale*. This scale is built entirely of whole steps. Note that the scale contains both the ♭5 and the ♯5.

C whole-tone

There are only two whole-tone scales. Because of its unusual construction, any of the notes in the scale may be considered the letter name of the scale. Between the two scales you have all the twelve possible letter names.

The C whole-tone scale may also be called the D whole-tone scale, E whole-tone scale, F♯ (G♭) whole-tone scale, G♯ (A♭) whole-tone scale, or B♭ (A♯) whole-tone scale. The scale may be used to improvise over any dominant seventh chord with a lowered and/or raised fifth whose root is one of the notes in the scale.

The other whole-tone scale is shown below.

The scale above may also be called by any of the notes in the scale and may be used to improvise over any dominant seventh chord with a lowered and/or raised fifth whose root is one of the notes in the scale.

Another scale that may be used to improvise over a dominant seventh flat-five chord is the Lydian ♭7 mode. The raised fourth in the scale is the enharmonic equivalent of the ♭5.

For a dominant seventh chord with a lowered ninth and/or a raised ninth the scale of choice is the half-step/whole-step diminished scale, or the whole-step/half-step diminished scale whose letter name is a half step higher than the root of the dominant seventh chord.

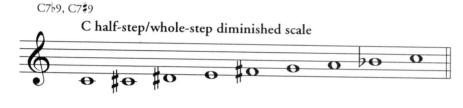

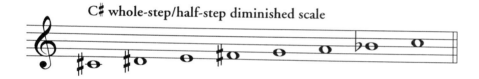

Dominant Seventh Chords with Flat-Nine and/or Sharp-Nine and Flat-Five

When the dominant seventh chord contains either a ♭9 and ♭5, or a ♯9 and ♭5, or any combination of both, the scale of choice is the whole-step/half-step diminished scale whose letter name is a half step higher than the root of the chord.

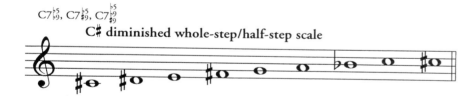

Dominant Seventh Flat-Five, Sharp-Five, Flat-Nine, Sharp Nine

When a dominant seventh chord contains all of the possible alterations ♭5, ♯5, ♭9, and ♯9, the scale of choice would be the super-Locrian mode. This scale contains all of the possible altered notes.

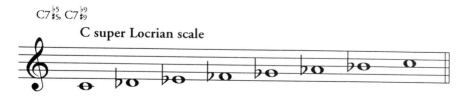

Another very useful scale that may be used over a dominant seventh chord containing all of the possible altered notes is the jazz minor scale. For a C7$^{\flat5\flat9}_{\sharp5\sharp9}$, use the jazz minor scale whose letter name is a half step higher than the root of the chord.

C7$^{\flat5}_{\sharp5}$, C7$^{\flat9}_{\sharp9}$

C♯ jazz minor scale

Note that the C super Locrian and the C♯ jazz minor have the same notes. The C super Locrian is a mode of the C♯ jazz minor scale.

We've just seen how scales are chosen to improvise over a particular dominant seventh chord containing altered notes. But even when a dominant seventh chord does not contain any altered notes, it is possible to use these scales in order to add more color to an otherwise bland scale. For example, to improvise over an unaltered G7 chord you would normally use the G Mixolydian mode. However, by using the G Lydian ♭7 scale you get a more colorful improvised solo. Using the A♭ diminished scale (whole-step/half-step) creates even more interest and using the A♭ jazz minor scale creates the most amount of color and interest. The more altered notes the scale provides, the farther away you are from the basic sound of the original chord, so great care must be taken in your choice of improvising scales.

THE BLUES SCALE

A scale that has no relationship with any particular chord but is probably the most used of all scales in pop and jazz music is known as the *blues scale*. The origin of the blues scale goes back to the early blues singers coming out of the Deep South in the early 1900s. In recordings of these early singers certain notes could be heard over and over again. These notes—the flatted third, flatted fifth, and flatted seventh of the major scale—became so characteristic of these early blues singers that the notes were called the *blue notes*. Eventually, when anybody wanted to sing or play the blues they would include these blue notes to give whatever they were singing or playing the blues feeling.

blue notes in the key of C

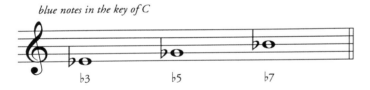

♭3   ♭5   ♭7

Over a period of time these blue notes combined with other notes from the scale have come to be known as the *blues scale*. The formula for creating the blues scale is to take the first, flatted third, fourth, flatted fifth, natural fifth, and the flatted seventh notes of the major scale.

C blues scale

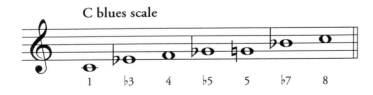

1   ♭3   4   ♭5   5   ♭7   8

The blues scale may be used to improvise over the entire twelve bars of the basic blues progression. For example, when playing the blues in the key of C you can use the above scale over the entire twelve bars. The scale may also be used with taste over any dominant seventh or minor seventh chords to get a blues feeling, even though the chords are not used in the twelve-bar blues structure.

Scale Application for II V I Progressions

When improvising over a II V I progression there are different approaches that may be taken. The simplest approach is to improvise over the entire progression using the scale of the I chord. For example, in a Dm7 G7 Cmaj7 progression you could use the C major scale over the entire three chords. This is known as playing in the key center.

C major scale

While the above approach is perfectly correct and will not offend the ear, there is a better approach. When improvising around a scale, there is a tendency to stress the basic notes of the I chord of that scale. Thus it would be best to improvise around the scale or mode of each chord in a progression. The Dorian mode would be used for the II chord, the Mixolydian mode for the V chord, and the major scale for the I chord.

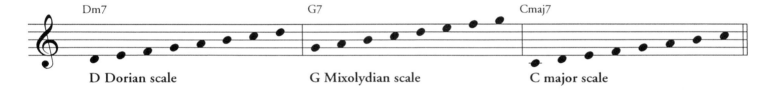

D Dorian scale   **G Mixolydian scale**   **C major scale**

Playing around the mode of each chord gives the solo melodic line a sense of movement since the harmony tends to be stressed. The line seems to flow and reach out until it finally arrives at the I chord with its major scale. It's a kind of tension and release feeling, with tension created in the II and V chords and release in the I chord.

Creating More Interest in the II V I Progression

Because the above II V I progression uses the same basic scale, even though you are starting from a different note for each chord, any improvised solo will sound rather bland and colorless. In order to create a greater degree of interest in our improvised solo, it would be better to use a completely different scale for each chord in the progression, as in the example below.

D Dorian scale   **G half-step/whole-step diminished scale**   **C Lydian scale**

Note that for the II chord we continue to use the Dorian mode but for the V chord we are using a half-step/whole-step diminished scale, even though the chord symbol, G7, does not call for a ♭5, ♭9, or ♯9. For the I chord we are using the Lydian scale, which creates a raised eleventh against the Cmaj7 chord. At this point it is important to understand that it is possible to add color to a chord by using scales such as those given on pages 100 through 102 even though the chord symbols do not call for the extended and altered notes that these scales produce.

The chord that is most receptive to a greater variety of scale choices is the V chord. The degree of tension may be controlled by the scale choice. Tension is created by the number of altered notes contained in the improvised line: the fewer altered notes the less the tension, the more altered notes the greater the tension. Below is a brief listing of some of the scales that may be played over a G7 chord. The numbers beneath each scale indicate the relationship of the scale degrees to the chord.

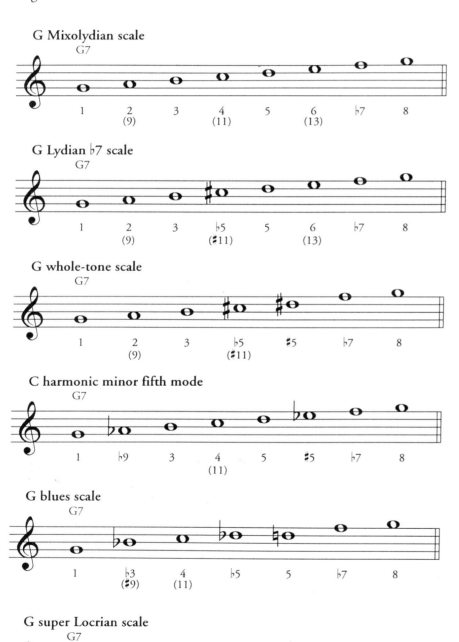

Note that a scale offering the same altered notes as the super Locrian is the jazz minor scale starting from a note a half step higher than the root of the V chord. For the G7 chord use the Ab jazz minor.

The I chord offers the least opportunity for scale choices. The obvious first choice is the major scale, but many jazz players prefer the Lydian mode because the raised fourth is the same as the raised eleventh which is the natural extended note of the major seventh chord.

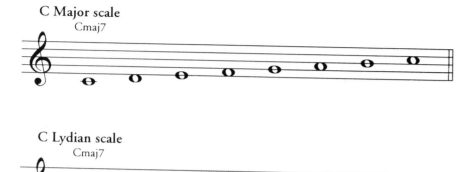

C Major scale

C Lydian scale

Improvising Scales for II V I Progressions in Minor

A simple approach to improvising over the II V I progression in minor is to use the scale of the I chord over the entire progression.

C harmonic minor scale

Following the example of using a different scale for each chord of the II V I progression in major, we will now do the same thing for the II V I in minor. Below is the progression in C harmonic minor with the modes given for each chord.

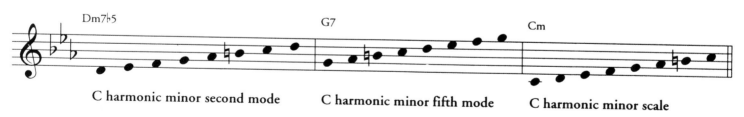

C harmonic minor second mode   **C harmonic minor fifth mode**   **C harmonic minor scale**

Although each chord in the above II V I progression has its own scale, it is basically all the same harmonic minor scale starting from a different note within the scale. Therefore, any improvised solo will have a rather bland sound, a sameness to the notes as you progress from chord to chord. To create a more interesting, colorful, tension-filled solo, it would be best to have a completely different scale for each chord.

The II chord in the minor key is a half diminished chord also called a minor seventh flat-five chord. This chord has three possible scale choices that may be used.

1. Locrian: The Locrian mode is the scale built from the seventh note of the major scale. Therefore, Dm7♭5 could be thought of as being derived from the E♭ major scale.

2. Locrian ♯2: This scale may be thought of as the same scale as above with the second note raised, or as being derived from the sixth note of the jazz minor scale. Therefore, Dm7♭5 would be derived from the sixth note of the F jazz minor scale.

3. Harmonic minor second mode: This scale is the second mode of the harmonic minor scale; therefore, Dm7♭5 could be derived from the second mode of the C harmonic minor scale. (This is probably the best choice.)

D Locrian scale

D Locrian ♯2 scale

C harmonic minor second mode

For the V chord in a minor progression there are at least five scale choices.

1. Super Locrian: This scale is derived from the jazz minor scale. Therefore, for a G7 chord in a minor key you may use the G super-Locrian scale (derived from the A♭ jazz minor scale).

2. Harmonic minor fifth mode: This scale is a mode of the harmonic minor scale. For the G7 chord use the fifth mode of the C harmonic minor scale.

3. Whole-tone: For the G7 chord in minor you can use a G whole-tone scale. This scale is built on whole steps.

4. Half-step/whole-step diminished: For the G7 chord in minor you may use the G half-step/whole-step diminished scale.

   If you wish to use the whole-step/half-step diminished scale be sure to build the scale, on the note a half step higher than the root of the V chord. For a G7 chord use the A♭ whole-step/half step diminished scale.

5. Blues scale. For the G7 chord in minor you may use the G blues scale.

G super Locrian scale

C harmonic minor fifth mode

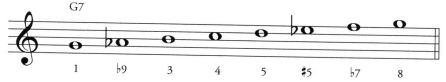

G whole-tone scale

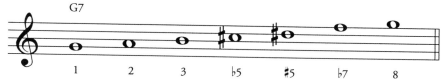

G half-step/whole-step diminished scale

A♭ whole-step/half-step diminished scale

G blues scale

In choosing an improvising scale for the I chord in a minor key, care should be taken to determine the quality of the I chord. For example, if you are playing over a Im(maj7) chord, you may use either the harmonic minor scale or jazz minor scale. However, if the I chord is just a minor seventh then either the pure (Aeolian) minor or the Dorian mode should be used.

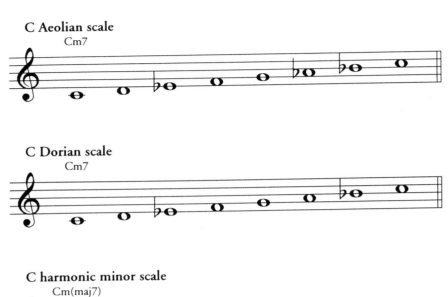

WORKSHEET

1. Write in the notes of the scale that would be best used for each of the chords in the following progressions.

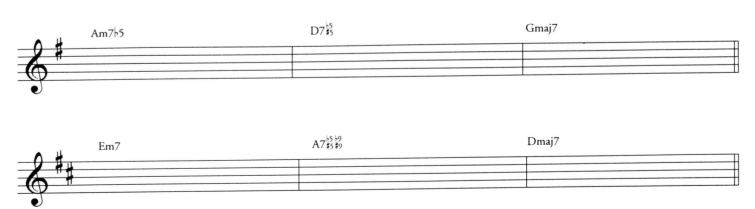

2. Write in the notes of the following scales.

Db Lydian b7 scale   E Mixolydian scale   B half-step/whole-step diminished scale

A jazz minor scale   F blues scale   F♯ Locrian scale

D whole-tone scale   B harmonic minor scale   C♯ whole-step/half-step diminished scale

INSTRUMENTAL EXERCISES

1. Play through each of the above scales. After you feel comfortable with each scale, improvise some one- and two-bar melodies through each scale.

2. Learn each of the above scales in every key. Improvise melodies on each scale in every key.

PENTATONIC SCALES

The *pentatonic scale,* although a very old scale, has been used more and more by jazz musicians and composers since the 1970s. People like Wayne Shorter, Freddie Hubbard, and Chick Corea have used pentatonic scales as the basis for their compositions. These scales have also been found to be very useful for improvising because they are rather simple to play and easy to learn.

The basic pentatonic scale is formed of the first, second, third, fifth, and sixth notes of the major scale.

Notice that in the above example, the C pentatonic scale would be very well suited to improvising against a C major chord, such as Cmaj7, Cmaj9, C6, or C$^6_9$. If the improviser wants to add a bit of tension to a solo, this could be acheived by using the D pentatonic against any of the above mentioned major chords. The F♯ in the D pentatonic scale would add the desired tension. Below we can see how the notes in the D pentatonic relate numerically to the C major seventh chord.

The greatest use of the pentatonic scale for creating tension is its use over a dominant type of chord, since it is dominant chords that usually seek greater degrees of tension. For example, below we see how a G♭ pentatonic scale would contribute to the C7 chord.

Notice that the G♭ pentatonic scale provides all of the possible altered notes to the C7 chord, the ♭5, ♯5, ♭9 and ♯9.

WORKSHEET

1. Write out the pentatonic scale starting from each note of the chromatic scale.

2. Write out the numerical relationship of each note in each pentatonic scale to each different chord type.

INSTRUMENTAL EXERCISES

1. At a piano, play a major seventh chord in the left hand and play through every possible pentatonic scale in the right hand. Notice which pentatonic scale offers the least tension and then which offers the greatest tension. Do this through every chord type.

2. Play pentatonic scales starting from every note on your instrument.

3. Using the following examples as models, play pentatonic scales all over your instrument.

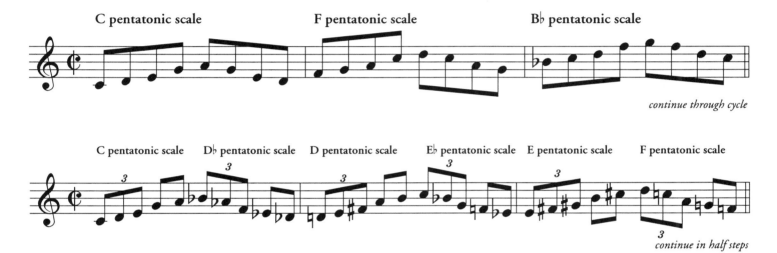